Bertha H. Leopold Buxton, William Wilhew Fenn

A Noble Name

Vol. I

Bertha H. Leopold Buxton, William Wilhew Fenn

A Noble Name
Vol. I

ISBN/EAN: 9783337046873

Printed in Europe, USA, Canada, Australia, Japan

Cover: Foto ©Andreas Hilbeck / pixelio.de

More available books at **www.hansebooks.com**

A NOBLE NAME:

A Novel.

By B. H. BUXTON
AUTHOR OF "JENNIE OF THE PRINCE'S," ETC.

AND

W. W. FENN
AUTHOR OF "HALF-HOURS OF BLIND MAN'S HOLIDAY," "THE
PALETTE AND THE PEN," ETC.

WITH OTHER STORIES

By W. W. FENN.

IN THREE VOLUMES.

VOL. I.

LONDON:
F. V. WHITE & Co., 31, SOUTHAMPTON STREET, STRAND.
1883.

Printed by KELLY & Co., London & Kingston.

PREFACE.

To me ·it has been a true, albeit a
somewhat sad pleasure, to prepare for
republication " A Noble Name," the tale
with which these volumes open.

It was written, alone of all the stories
here brought together, in conjunction
with Mrs. B. H. Buxton, author of
" Jennie of the Prince's."

She had made her mark some time
before our acquaintance began, and although she had always ample employment
for her clever pen, she was never too
busy during the period of our brief friend-
ship, to aid me with her bright suggestions
and willing hand.

Coming one day upon the early chapters

of this tale, she insisted on our working on it together; I gladly consented: for when and under what circumstances does not a blind man welcome real help and sympathy?

She entered warmly into the scheme, and so, after many a pleasant evening's labour, " A Noble Name " was completed, —with what success others must decide.

But only a few days after the last words in the last chapter were penned, the busy brain and tender heart of my kindly, genial fellow-worker were at rest. On the evening of the 30th of March, 1881, without pain, without warning, spared all sorrowful farewells, she passed, in a moment, away.

A more sympathetic friend it would be hard to find, and in our home she leaves a blank which my wife and I shall never cease to feel.

I have only to add that the short

stories contained in these volumes are similar in character to those which have found such favour with the readers of " Half-Hours of Blind Man's Holiday."

W. W. FENN.

GREAT MARLBOROUGH STREET,
January, 1883.

CONTENTS.

A NOBLE NAME.

CHAPTER I.

A CATASTROPHE.

"GLORIOUS! positively glorious! The only suggestions of discord, in the harmony of peace and beauty, are the shrill voices of those children at play below. Poor little imps! Perhaps noise is as essential to their happiness as perfect tranquillity is to mine!"

Arriving at this charitable conclusion, Hubert Northcroft sighs profoundly; but he does not look at all sad as he stretches himself at full length upon the elastic carpet provided by generous Dame Nature, and leisurely proceeds to

fill and light his long china-bowled pipe.
He is a good-looking man; indeed, he
may fairly be described as handsome,
and though far on the road to forty,
is evidently in his prime. He wears a
loose coat of brown velveteen, and a
broad-brimmed Tyrolean hat is set on his
head with a *nonchalant* air, which suits
the man admirably. His bright blue
eyes betray a mirthful spirit, which
oddly enough is at variance with a
melancholy note in his musical voice.
His utterance is slow and deliberate;
he has a habit of sighing profoundly,
and yet he is of a contented nature, and
thoroughly cheerful disposition. It is
time, not trouble, which is leaving silver
traces in his thick brown beard and
curly hair.

The first part of the speech above

recorded is addressed to Nature, who certainly merits the apostrophe, for she is showing herself at her brightest and fairest here. The grumbling *addendum* is intended for the sympathetic ear of Hubert's wife, who sits on the grass by his side, plying her knitting-needles with an amount of energy that bespeaks an active temperament. Mrs. Northcroft is decidedly a handsome woman still; though not much younger than her husband. She also has " worn well." Her soft brown eyes are clear and bright, her hair is plentiful, and, as yet, without a trace of the snowy passage of Time. Mrs. Northcroft is energetic by nature ; Hubert is indolent. She acts, while he pauses to reflect, and her promptitude and rapid decision invariably come to aid his more deliberate method of thought and action.

Most travellers are familiar with the scene on which this pleasant-looking couple are gazing. The picturesque village of Meyringen lies just below the grassy knoll on which they have seated themselves. It is a lovely evening towards the end of June, 1850, and the setting sun is already sending a rosy flush to warm the dazzling whiteness of the eternal snow-peaks on the horizon.

The shrill voices of the children playing on the slope below are the only sounds that jar upon the sense of universal peace and quiet; for the distant thud-like echo of the great Reichenbach Fall, and the occasional tinkle of cow and goat-bells harmonize so pleasantly with time and place, as to create no disturbing element.

"It's that small creature with the yellow hair, the baby of the party, that makes

the greatest noise," observed Mrs. Northcroft, after an interval of silence. She
has been eagerly watching the merry group
beneath her, and this is the conclusion she
arrives at.

"Look, Hugh; is she not a little darling, I wish she would come up here. Her
hair is just the colour of Lina's. I wonder
if her eyes are brown, too."

"I wish our Lina was as active as that
pretty romp," says Hubert, sending the
blue tobacco smoke upwards in delicate
cloudlets, and leaning over to get a better
view of the children below.

"What a contrast that nimble fairy
presents to the rest of the vulgar brats,"
he says. "This Canton is justly famed
for the squat ugliness of its female popu-
lation, and that makes a golden-haired
baby a welcome and delightful exception

to an odious rule.   I often pondered on
Nature's want of generosity to the Swiss
girls, when I was painting here as a
student years ago.   I little dreamt then
that the time would come when I should
have a lovely wife and daughter of my
own.   Heigho!"   Hubert's customary
sigh ends his complacent oration, and his
blue eyes rest on his comely wife with
exceeding tenderness.   "I suppose we had
better go in and see after our own baby
now," he adds, puffing more smoke into
the air, and evidently most reluctant to
move, though he suggests the desirability
of doing so.   "What would I not give to
see Lina as merry and active as that child
below.   Do you think she is really better
for the change, wife?"   The sigh that
follows this question in due course is
fraught with a certain anxiety this time,

and something that might be a tear glitters in Hubert's eyes.

"I hope so," says his wife, promptly, and reassuringly. "Lina's health, I think, has improved every day, since we have settled in this glorious mountain air. I fancy she seems to benefit by every breath she draws up here. Do not let us hurry home just yet, Hugh. You know how attentive and devoted nurse is, and I am anxious about you, my dear. I want you to glean fresh inspiration from this magnificent sunset. Take a good long look at it. I confess to being a little disappointed that you have not even begun a sketch this afternoon; but now if you wish it, I will pack up your 'traps' and we will hope for as fine a day to-morrow. Then I think you ought to accomplish something."

"*Che sarà sarà*," says Hubert, dubiously,

and his wife busies herself in collecting the sketching paraphernalia which litters the grass. "Thanks, my dear," he remarks, presently, quite content to leave all exertion to his wife, "I knew I should do no good this afternoon; I might just as well have left all my traps at home. Painting out of doors is very troublesome. You must be thoroughly at your ease and undisturbed to do any good work at all."

Looking at Hubert, it seems impossible that he is ever otherwise than at his ease, and the excuse for idleness appears untenable. While Mrs. Northcroft is engaged with her packing, her husband's attention wanders from the wide landscape back to the children below, who have formed a ring and are dancing around the fair-haired child standing in the centre. The game evidently entitles her to some show of adulation; for her companions bow the knee like courtiers, while she stands in calm superiority, until the pantomime of the others leads to a little merry burst of song from her. Her sweet child-voice rises pure and clear in the still air, and to Hubert the piping treble of the Swiss melody sounds delicious.

"When you have done packing, Letty, I wish you would go and catch that musical fairy and bring her up here. I should like to know what that song is about, and I should like to see if she is as picturesque as she appears at this distance. Perhaps I might paint her. I think she would make a pretty picture if I took time and trouble about it, and I have nothing particular to do here. What a ruddy contrast to our pale maiden at home, eh, wife?"

This time again Hubert's sigh is regretful; for his only child, as has been hinted, is very delicate and causes her parents constant anxiety. Mrs. Northcroft, conscious of the gloom settling on her husband, hastens to divert his attention by obeying his behest. She is lithe of limb, strong and active, and runs nimbly down the slope to where the childish party is assembled, and after a short confabulation with the eldest of them, she returns, leading the " fairy " by the hand. Hubert has watched all her proceedings, with a lazy patient air of interest, so she leads the little girl towards him, he raises himself, and leisurely taking his pipe in one hand, he stretches the other towards the small child, whom he welcomes with a beaming smile, and addresses in perfect German. He has spent so many years of his life abroad, that he has mastered many continental languages.

"What fine games you have been playing all this long sunny afternoon, little one," he says pleasantly. "Do you think you can give me a kiss now, to thank me for not scolding you when you made such a terrible noise down there? You disturbed me so much that I could not work at all. Are you not sorry?"

The child laughs saucily. "You must play too," she lisps. "All work makes Peter discontent!"

Hubert is intensely amused by this gravely delivered speech.

"This is Miss Precocious," he says to his wife in English.

"Speak ee-ze Engliss," announces the "fairy." She has a sweet, merry face, and looks very kissable. She stretches up her small hands now and begins to play with the great bunch of seals and trinkets attached to Hubert's watch-chain. He regards her attentively the while, and says to his wife, " She is a juvenile Hebe. What limbs she has, and what a bonnie face. Pity soap seems an unknown quantity in her toilette arrangements. I should like to see her properly groomed, her hair is as silky as Lina's and quite as bright ; but what a tangle ! "

" I am sure she has no mother to look after her, poor mite," says Mrs. North-croft, with ready compassion. " I shall go into the village and inquire about her belongings. How old art thou, *liebe Kleine?* "

" I am three years old to-day ; that is why I was made into a birthday queen," says *Kleine*, with an air of conscious importance.

" Just Lina's age," remarks Hubert, pondering. " And where dost thou live?" he asks, presently.

" Why down there!" she says, promptly, and points to an isolated châlet beyond the village beneath them.

" Is that your parents' house?" asks Hubert.

" Father's house," says the child; "dear mammy's gone away to heaven." The little lip quivers and sudden tears cloud the bright eyes.

> "The tear down childhood's cheek that flows
> Is like the dew-drop on the rose;
> When next the summer breeze comes by,
> And shakes the bush, the flower is dry."

" You were right, as usual, wife," says Hubert, and stoops again to kiss the pretty blonde head.

" And what is your name, Kleine? "

" 'Lisbeth Freundlein," says she, nothing loth to answer questions, while she is permitted to play with those marvellous trinkets on the watch-chain.

" 'Lisbeth Freundlein — Freundlein — Freundlein," repeats Hubert, making the harmonious syllables into a phrase of song.

" It is a quaint euphonious name," he says to his wife, and she replies " It suits the dainty maid exactly."

Hubert has lifted the child on his arm now, and her head nestles against his shoulder with the ease of perfect confidence.

" Adieu, *liebe 'Lisbeth, liebe, liebe Kleine*, 'Lisbeth Freundlein," he whispers. " It is time to go home now. Will you run down to your friends, birthday queen ? " As he speaks he glances at her playfellows on the lower slope.

But what is happening there?

A sudden stampede has occurred. The children are rushing away in all directions, scurrying down the further slopes as fast as their feet will carry them. Away, away towards the road which traverses the valley and leads to the Grimsel Pass. Along this path a man is running at full speed. He shouts vociferously, he waves his arms, and seems carried on by a very whirlwind of excitement.

" 'Lisbeth must run too," cries the child decisively, and slipping out of Hubert's arm she in her turn scuds away, down one slope after another.

" What can have happened to cause all this commotion?" says Mrs. Northcroft anxiously, and both she and her husband watch the proceedings of that eager, excited messenger, who is gesticulating fiercely as he tells his tidings to the interested villagers in the street below.

The men, when they have heard him, disappear within their houses, only to return a few minutes later, laden with poles, ropes, and ladders.

Thus armed, eight or ten of them return with the herald of danger, and in a body they hurry away towards the Grimsel Pass. The women and children follow at greater or less speed.

Hubert has taken the burden of traps from his wife's willing hand. "Let us go and inquire what has happened," he says; but it is the lady who sets forth at a brisk pace, while he follows leisurely.

"I do hope it is nothing very dreadful," she says, looking grave. "You follow,

Hugh, dear. I must hasten to see if I can be of any use."

" Some of those fool-hardy climbers come to grief again, no doubt," says Hubert, sighing in commiseration. "What a deplorable mania people have for getting a-top of every mountain they see. And it all looks so much better and is so much more satisfactory from a reasonable distance. I should like to put a chain round their legs when they talk of . . . ."

Hubert, who had been soliloquizing in his usual meditative fashion, now perceives that his wife is already quite out of earshot, and actually prepares himself to catch her up by quickening his easy stride.

They reach the long, narrow street, the one street of the village, just as the last rays of the setting sun fade from the surrounding snow-peaks, leaving them pale and ghastly, like dead embers of the great crimson fire, which but a moment ago had expired on their crests. The grey shades of evening are creeping upwards from the valley, and approach the sides of the mighty mountains tenderly.

But the peace which usually settles down upon the homes of the frugal Switzers at this hour, is wanting to-night. The villagers are met in the street, the women's voices sound shrill and eager, wild exclamations and sharp replies rise above the murmur of the expectant crowd, and at the entrance to the courtyard of their hotel, the Northcrofts find that the hubbub is greatest, and opine that here at last the nature of the catastrophe will be revealed to them.

CHAPTER II.

IN crossing the Grimsel, one of a party of adventurous climbers had fallen over a precipice. That is all the news the Northcrofts manage to obtain on their return to the hotel. The guide, who had been sent down to the village for assistance had not stayed to give any details. He realized the urgency of what was required of him too thoroughly to lose any time in explanations, and he may have been animated by the conviction that the practical aid he carried to those in distress would avert fatal consequences after all. Hours must elapse before the relief party

c 2

could return to Meyringen and bring more
detailed accounts of the calamity which
had befallen one of the travellers. Mrs.
Northcroft, having brought little Lina to
father for a good-night kiss and blessing,
expressed an earnest desire to sit up in the
nursery all night, so that she might be
dressed and ready to help whenever the
sufferer should be carried home ; but
Hubert vehemently opposed this "folly,"
and, by dint of quiet coaxing, persuaded
his energetic wife to go to bed and leave
philanthropy to others on this occasion.
Hubert slept soundly all night; but his
wife listened anxiously for the footsteps
that never came. Towards morning she
fell into an uneasy slumber and dreamed
she was back in her cosy artistic home in
Munich again, and that she rushed to the
rescue only just in time to catch little Lina

in her arms, who was falling out of the nursery window.

Mr. and Mrs. Northcroft had journeyed to Switzerland by easy stages and with a double purpose. The old doctor recommended mountain air for delicate Lina, and Alpine scenery was the one thing needful (so he said) to make Hubert attack his work with renewed vigour again. During the previous spring and summer he had painted some admirable landscapes in Tyrol; but the autumn and winter were spent in making plans, and his wife ardently desired to see these visions assume a more tangible shape at last. The happy trio had but lately arrived at Meyringen, and so early in the season there were but few tourists abroad. Thirty years ago their number, at the most crowded part of the year, was far less than in these days of mountain railroads and easy locomotion, and it was quite possible to enjoy peace and quiet, even at the principal hotel of this, one of the chief starting-points for Alpine climbers.

No further news of the accident reached Mrs. Northcroft in her room, and when she went downstairs she was glad to find that she and her husband were the sole occupants of the large *salle à manger;* for Karl, the active *kellner,* would be able to devote himself to them and could surely tell them all the news of which he was the chief purveyor.

"A letter, wife!" cries Hubert, in evident astonishment, as he takes up an envelope that lies beside his breakfast plate. "A letter from home—my old home, I mean, and forwarded from Munich by Schmidt."

" A letter from your brother Stephen ? "
asks Mrs. Northcroft, surprised in her turn,
but not pleasantly, and as she speaks there
is a slight compression of her full, sensitive
lips. " What can he want from you,
Hugh, after these years of silence——? ' "

" You were going to say *neglect,* wife,"
remarks Hubert, with his easy smile and
deliberate tone of conviction. " Well, if
he has neglected me, *voilà* the *amende
honorable.* Behold ! one, two, three sheets,
six pages, and all clearly written. Dear
wife, take pity on me. I hate reading
letters, as you know. I wonder what
could have induced Stephen to take so
much trouble. Do you think it was done
to give me trouble in my turn ? "

" Hardly," says Mrs. Northcroft, smiling
pleasantly at her husband's appeal, and the
melancholy look which accompanies it.

"Take your coffee, Hugh, and I will read you the wonderful epistle, while mine cools.

"Pineridge Priory, Torshire,

"June 12th.

"Dear Hubert,—Yesterday, I read in the *Torshire Chronicle* with strangely mixed feelings, an account purporting to be extracted from the *Cologne Gazette*, which gives an elaborate description of a landscape painted by you and now said to be publicly exhibited in Munich. I repeat, I read this account with mixed feelings, but I must at once admit that I was not agreeably impressed. For though the critic quoted spoke in such laudatory terms of your work that I could not fail to be somewhat gratified, I certainly should have desired that *our* name might never be publicly associated with any such labours as yours ; indeed, it caused me a pang to think that the editor of our leading county paper should have the power to draw the eyes of the world to this derogatory fact—here, on my very threshold. I still maintain, as I have ever done, that one descended from so proud a line of ancestors as ours, is degraded by pursuing the trade of a painter. Diplomacy, the Army, or the Church, can alone afford such opportunities for distinction as befit a younger son of the Northcrofts. However successful you may eventually be in the calling you have chosen to adopt, I shall never cease to regret that your tastes should have led you to so lowly—I may even say so unworthy a pursuit."

Mrs. Northcroft pauses, and that odd compression of her lips is more evident

than before. " Am I to read any more of
these insults, Hugh?" she asks, her fine
eyes flashing and an angry frown con-
tracting her brow.

" If you please, my dear," says Hubert,
with a weary sigh and an amused smile.
" There must be some motive for so much
brotherly display of interest. Let me hear
the rest of the good wishes and back-
handed compliments."

With an impatient gesture, Mrs. Northcroft continues—

" As you certainly have made some
mark, however, I thought I should be
wanting in that courtesy which I esteem
my first duty to friend and foe, if I failed
to acknowledge what *you* no doubt consider a triumph. I cannot honestly say
that I *congratulate* you ; but I wish you

to know that I am aware of your *success*, such as it is. I address my letter to Munich; but as I have not heard from you since you wrote to tell me of your marriage, and the subsequent birth of your daughter, it is doubtful whether this epistle will ever reach you. I hope it may do so, however; for I shall be glad to hear that you and yours are well, and I also wish to assure you that if you at any time feel inclined to return to England, a welcome and a suite of rooms are ready for you in the old home. That at least is unaltered. It looks much as it did in the life-time of our honoured parents. I always objected to change, as you know, but in these levelling days it requires a strong will and a resolute hand to ward off the baneful spirit of innovation.

" You will be sorry to hear that I can

give you no better account of my son's sight. Indeed, the first prediction of the oculists consulted in his infancy is realised; he is absolutely blind now. This is a source of infinite trouble to me, for he is a handsome intelligent boy, and in course of time might have become a creditable heir to the high position his name entitles him to take. But alas! what chance is there for him? He has to be educated through his sense of hearing, and his fingers are his eyes. Instead of being taught to use the cricket-bat, or ride to hounds, he will grow up as helpless and useless as a baby, and even a daughter might eventually be better able to manage these great estates, and to uphold our noble name in the county, than my unfortunate son will ever be. He does not appear to suffer any pain, or to be personally distressed by his affliction. This seems the more extraordinary to me, as I find his helplessness and inactivity a continual source of grief and vexation. Let me hear from you soon, and believe me,

" Your affectionate brother,

" STEPHEN NORTHCROFT."

" A very affectionate brother, eh, wife? " says Hubert, setting down his empty coffee-cup, and sighing as he smiles ; " and he actually wrote all that because the sight of my name in a newspaper reminded him of my existence ; well, well! "

" I think it is bad—bad," says Mrs. Northcroft, sharply. " He has surely lived long enough to know better. Why does he not enlarge his cramped provincial ideas? Why does he not learn that painting is a noble and elevating pursuit?

Why does he . . ? . . . Why does he not love and pity that poor dear blind boy of his ? "

Hubert interrupts her with more eagerness of speech and mind than he is wont to show.

" Why?　Because Stephen Northcroft is as little able to understand and sympathise with his son and his affliction as with his brother the artist, and with an artist's aspirations.　Diplomacy?　A fine diplomatist I should have made, indeed.　You know, Letty, what a capital hand I am at managing my own affairs.　Eh ? "

" Yes ; I know," she answers, laying a caressing hand on his.　" You have not even learnt to check your own bills yet, and if I did not look after you, you would always pay anything that anybody asked you."

" So long as I had the money, I certainly should," says Hubert. " It would save a lot of trouble in the end and avoid all sorts of discussion.

" The alternative your generous brother suggests is hardly a suitable one either," says the loving wife, looking proudly at her husband. " Your figure would never have appeared to such advantage in a shell jacket as it does in your painting coat."

" I cannot fancy myself in a cut-throat collar, either," says Hubert, putting his hand under his beard and grasping the bare muscular throat which rises above the artistic turn-down strip of linen.

" I fear this aristocratic, high and mighty Sir Stephen will have to make the best of his noble name being dabbled in paint, after all," says Mrs. Northcroft, and with some bitterness she adds: "Your brother writes as if you were a house-painter, instead of ranking you among the first of living landscape painters."

"Ah! there's no knowing what *1* may do with a fond, encouraging wife to pat me on the back," says Hubert, chuckling; "but there is little doubt that Stephen does consider a picture painter, and a putty and glazier chap as very nearly akin. Well, wife, if we ever do make up our minds to go to England, we will stay at the Priory, and convert this in-artistic heathen, but that won't be for some time yet."

At this moment, Karl, the dapper little *kellner*, makes his appearance to clear away the breakfast things. The *Herr-schaften* were too much engaged with their correspondence to heed him when he brought the coffee ; but now he has a chance of imparting the news he has just heard in the courtyard.

"The *Herrschaften* will be grieved to hear," he says, speaking in his own tongue, "that the bad news brought last night was only too true. A life was lost on the pass, but not the life of one of the strangers; it was a guide who was killed." And then, with exceeding volubility and lively pantomime, Karl relates the tragedy as he has just heard it.

"It was in saving the life of a reckless —alas! a too fool-hardy Englishman that the brave guide was killed. The gentleman had set his heart on plucking a spray of *edelweis*, which only grows at a certain altitude, and perceiving the flower in question, he determined to defy the cautions of his guide, and risk crossing a certain ledge which he was told was dangerous. When he had reached the spot where the flower grew, he saw a finer specimen beneath him and he bent over to seize that also; but the place was a horrible one — quite a precipice they tell me. I do not know, I never visit these traps for human lives myself. Of course this obstinate Englander lost his head and he became too terrified to move. His guide, seeing his distress, made haste to go to his rescue; but the ledge of rock is narrow, and there is not room for two upon it. Then the guide, who was a brave noble spirit—ah! I knew him well—he was full of a great courage —balances himself on a sharp point of overhanging rock—a piece like a knife, they say—ugh! and he leans over, holds a helping hand to the traveller, and so saves him ; but as he himself turns, his foot slips. Ah ! . ."

Here Karl pauses for a moment, noting the effect he produces with critical appreciative eyes.

" And he falls ? " cries Mrs. Northcroft, whose face has become very pale.

"That would not have mattered, not at all, Madame," says Karl, enjoying her emotion ; "for, of course, the poor fellow is tied by a rope around his waist. But, ah ! the rope is rotten, and the jerk he gives it when he almost loses his balance breaks it in two, and he falls, falls thousands of feet — down, down, only to be picked up, crushed—bleeding—dead."

" Mamma, mamma, why are you so frightened ? " lisps a small voice at Mrs. Northcroft's elbow, and loving arms are lifted to the mother's neck. It is little

Lina who has crept into the *salle-à-manger* unperceived, and who knows too little German to follow the *patois* in which Karl relates his tragic history.

"The guide, he leaves a poor little girl—a pretty child with hair like your little Fraulein's there," says Karl, sorrowfully. "And now that poor orphan is all alone in the world."

"What was his name, poor fellow—poor fellow?" asked Hubert, compassionately.

"Oscar Freundlein," answers Karl. "A friend of mine, and a noble man in his life—good, brave, and true; indeed he deserved a better fate. And now that little orphan is without kith or kin, and almost friendless in the world."

"Not friendless, surely, while we can help," says Hubert to his wife in English.

And as though realizing the loneliness of the orphan child, he takes his own little daughter in his arms and briefly tells her the story ; then he kisses her tenderly and adds, " We will be the lonely maiden's friends, won't we, Lina darling ? "

And Lina, with her gentle smile and her old-fashioned grave manner, answers :

" We will do whatever you think best, dear father."

CHAPTER III

THE fame of the great picture painted
by Hubert Northcroft, a faint echo
of which had reached England, and the
ears of his brother Stephen, was but the
first of a series of triumphs. Cheered
and encouraged by the reception of more
ambitious efforts on his part, Hubert continued to paint and exhibit with repeated
and increasing success. Some record of
his achievements always found its way
into the *Torshire Chronicle* now, and thus
came under the notice of the owner of
Pineridge, and was remembered, if not
remarked upon, by that austere person-

age. Having broken the ice of estrangement by recognising his brother's existence in the letter received at Meyringen, Sir Stephen felt that he had amply fulfilled the requirements of that courtesy which he made a point of practising towards " friend and foe." Hubert responded to this considerate advance on the part of the county magnate by a short letter in which he stated that his time was fully occupied by the pursuit of that profession which was now a joy as well as a necessity to him. For the present he said he could neither spare the time nor the money required for a journey to England. In the course of a few years, however, he hoped to re-visit his old home and would then thankfully avail himself of his brother's proffered hospitality. To write a letter required a far greater effort than Hubert

at any time felt himself equal to; but that
useful help-mate of his was as ready with
her pen as with any other assistance
required by her indolent and exacting lord
in all practical matters. He was always
at work now; he painted all day and every
day. What more natural than that she
should undertake all other duties for him?

Sir Stephen was inclined to resent the
fact that Hubert dictated his letters instead
of writing them; but then the elder brother
always cavilled at the short-comings of the
younger. He read the frequent accounts
of Hubert's artistic successes in the same
deprecating spirit in which he received the
first mention of his brother's name in print.
The fact that a Northcroft had turned
painter was in itself derogatory; but the
younger Northcroft's distinction in his
profession made the thought of it less dis-

tasteful after a time. In some measure Hubert's success now began to atone for the years of idleness, the careless Bohemian existence he had led during his protracted stay on the Continent. To the grave owner of Pineridge, the time his brother spent abroad appeared recklessly dissipated, and he never anticipated any but bad results from it. It was that laudatory paragraph in the *Torshire Chronicle* which first opened his prejudiced eyes to the fact that some sort of distinction might be obtained *even* by a painter. The subsequent accounts of Hubert's reception at the court of Bavaria, and of visits paid to his studio by Serene Highnesses, Titled Excellencies, and other exalted personages, served to reconcile Sir Stephen still more to the profession his brother had adopted. But even in these pleasing details the proud senior found a source of shame and annoyance; for they were followed by statements of the important commissions undertaken by the artist, and the high prices he now obtained for his work.

To Sir Stephen the fact that his brother actually worked for money, was paid for the labour of his brain and hands, was intolerable. It appeared a positive degradation, and painting seemed even less dignified than trading. In the latter case a merchant simply handled money; in the former, he actually worked for it like any mechanic.

Time, the universal healer, and Hubert's continued prosperity, served, in due course, to overcome the first violence of Sir Stephen's displeasure, and finally he came to allude to "my brother the artist," or "my brother's successful pic-

ture," with something approaching satisfaction.

It was twenty years now since young
Hubert, in a fit of desperate rebellion
against his exacting father and prim
dictatorial elder brother, had fled from
his home and his country, and sought
refuge from the tyranny which bound
him hand and foot, in the delightful
freedom of the *laisser-aller* existence led
by art students on the Continent. The
news of his father's death and his
brother's inheritance of the title and
property did not tempt Hubert to return
to England ; but the small patrimony he
now inherited as younger son enabled
him to live in comparative comfort, and
to pursue with ease the profession to
which his taste and inclination led him.
The monetary arrangements were con-

ducted by Sir Stephen's solicitor and bankers in London, and their agents in Paris, and there was little or no communication between the brothers for years. It was the announcement in the *Times* of Sir Stephen's marriage, with the daughter of a neighbouring landowner and J.P. of Torshire, that brought a letter of congratulation from Hubert, and soon after this epistle had been answered, the artist again broke the silence which was lengthening into estrangement, by the announcement of his own marriage to Letitia Bryant, the daughter of a retired English officer, who lived in Munich on half pay. This communication was followed a year after by another letter in which Hubert, proud and exulting, informed the head of the family that a daughter had been born to the house of Northcroft. As Sir Stephen answered but coldly to these ebullitions of feeling, a fresh silence ensued, and all the brothers knew of one another's doings were the important facts that both were married and each had a child. Joy in the advent of an heir at Pineridge however had been damped at once by the sad revelation that baby Philip, whose birth had cost his mother her life, was likely to lose his eyesight before he could know what eyesight was.

The next news that the wanderer Hubert received from England was in the letter which we have read, and which followed him on his Swiss tour, and contained those left-handed congratulations which provoked the ire of high-spirited Letitia. Formal as it was, that epistle had certainly narrowed the breach between the brothers; and during the six years following its receipt, letters occasionally passed between them.

Those six years had been spent by Hubert in ceaseless and arduous work; for though he lost much time in theorising, and more still in grumbling amiably, he managed to work as well. The holiday he spent in Switzerland seemed to have given him fresh impetus, and the cheering companionship of his high-minded, energetic wife encouraged him to persevere now, where he would erst have yielded to his natural indolence. He was thoroughly acclimatized in Munich by this time, and it was from this quaint home of Teutonic art that the Englishman sent forth those pictures to the exhibitions in Paris, Vienna, and other Continental centres, which, in time, secured for him an European reputation.

It is a bright, clear, January morning, between six and seven years since we first saw our friends on the slopes at Meyringen. It is frosty, keen, and inspiriting out of doors, snug and comfortable within the capacious light studio, heated as it is by the china-tiled stove in the far corner. Close by the fire, Mrs. Northcroft is sitting, busy with her knitting as usual. (How many pairs of socks has she made since first we beheld her thus occupied among the Swiss mountains?) Hubert, palette and mahlstick in one hand, brush in the other, stands before the large, half-covered canvas to which he devotes every hour of the now precious daylight.

" This clump of firs in the foreground, and the path that leads away towards the stream, always remind me of Torshire," he says, as he examines his work. " When I was a small boy, I used to go fishing in a brook something like that, which is within a mile of the Priory."

"I wonder if I shall ever see your old home, Hugh," says his wife, smiling up at him ; " I know you would like me to visit all your old haunts with you."

" Indeed I should, wife," said he, straightening himself and adjusting his palette ; " and there are times when the thought of my brother all alone in that great house with his poor blind boy, makes me quite melancholy. It does seem sad that Stephen and I, brothers as we are, and the only two representatives left out of a once large and united family, should be permanently estranged. He, living in England in solitary grandeur, I, leading a busy, happy life in the home made so cheerful for me by you, wife, and our Fairy. I really think it is quite time now that we should take some active steps towards a reconciliation, and since Stephen has offered us hospitality in the old home, let us accept it. I think I can manage to get away this year, and as soon as I receive the money from Graf von Stein for this commission, I should like to try my hand at English landscape for a change. Let us settle to leave Munich in May, wife. Lina will enjoy the journey, too, and her blithe companionship is sure to be a pleasure and comfort to that unfortunate blind lad. It positively makes my heart ache to think of him." This speech is followed by a profound sigh, of course, and Hubert's blue eyes turn towards his wife in wistful appeal. There is more white hair on his head and in his beard, and a slight increase of *embonpoint* and wrinkles, but there is also the same *négligé* style of attire, and quite as bright and kind an expression on the pleasant face as ever.

" I fear you and your brother are not at all likely to agree, after all these years," says Mrs. Northcroft, anxiously. " Your views on all subjects seem so dissimilar now."

" They always were, my dear," says Hubert. " And upon my word it is only natural," he adds with a laugh, " that Stephen should be horrified with my mode of life. The sole aim of his existence has always been to keep up the dignity of the Northcroft family, and my erratic existence and devotion to a profession have outraged his fine old provincial prejudices, of course. It was trying for him no doubt that I, his only brother, should prefer a continental life and the society of slovenly artists, with long beards and short pipes, to the stilted respectability of the county folks with whom it is his 'pride and pleasure' to associate. Oh! Letty, what a stupid lot those provincial magnates seemed to me! Never a word to say except about horse-racing, fox-hunting—*scent*, coverts, coveys, turnips, or partridges! Can human ingenuity devise a more terrific ordeal of boredom, eh?"

"And you are willing to expose yourself to such suffering again, Hugh, and all for your aristocratic brother's sake?" Mrs. Northcroft looks up with a questioning smile, and her husband goes near to where she is sitting and possesses himself of her

E 2

hands to the serious detriment of her knitting.

"I long to show *you* the old home, the old ancestral home of the Northcrofts, as Stephen so proudly calls it," he says, and looks tenderly into the quiet earnest face of the woman he honestly loves and respects ; "it certainly was a wise dispensation of Providence," he says meditatively, " that gave Stephen the priority in our distinguished family. He is the right man in the right place. The title and the estate both fit him admirably. Responsibility is the salt of his serious life. I could never have kept the place up properly, or the tenants, or the accounts, in proper order; but I admire the man who can, and who does do all these things, and I really believe that he is mollified about my Bohemian tendencies, since people have begun to make such a fuss about my pictures. We shall get on better now than ever before, my dear anxious wife. And I should like you to write to Stephen this very day, and propose our visit to him. Letters are no trouble to you, are they?"

"If I do write, I had surely better explain the whole truth to him, Hugh," says Mrs. Northcroft, with a rapid glance towards her husband, which looks almost like entreaty.

"Tut, tut, my dear," says he promptly. "What is the use of bothering. You don't know the man, or you would never suggest any sort of explanation. Leave well alone!"

"Ah! but will it be well?" queries Mrs. Northcroft, and this time the sigh —and a very deep one—is hers.

"Here is our darling, our Fairy and

Sunshine!" exclaims Hubert, evidently relieved as he hears the patter, patter of Lina's little feet on the polished floor of the corridor without.

"And how went school, and the lessons, and the pastors, and masters, and mississes?" he asks the little one, whose rosy cheeks glow with health and frost, and who jumps into his arms with all a child's glad *abandon* at a real home-coming.

"My darling—my sweet little Lina," he says, kissing her fondly. "Tell me, would you like to go a long journey with mother and father—a journey to old England?"

"Oh! yes; yes; yes;" cries the child, delighted. All children love change and look forward to it with happiest anticipations. Of the trio in the studio at

Munich, Mrs. Northcroft is the only one who thinks of the journey to England with unspoken, but ever-increasing doubts and fears.

CHAPTER IV

ALTHOUGH Sir Stephen Northcroft received the announcement of his brother's intended visit to the home of his fathers with more complacency than might have been expected some years previously, the subsequent telegram, which told of Hubert Northcroft's safe arrival in Dover, produced considerable trepidation in the well-balanced mind of the baronet. A meeting between brothers so long separated, and whose parting had been by no means amicable, could not fail to agitate a person with so profound a regard for conventionalities. Sir Stephen, after much hesitation and with many misgivings, had resolved to acknowledge his brother's success in that derogatory profession of his; but the general invitation to the Priory, with which he had wound up more than one of his " courteous " letters of late, had been but an expression of polite consideration, and he was greatly surprised and not a little perplexed, when, after a lapse of years, he found that invitation cordially accepted, and heard to his dismay that the Hubert family would probably appear at Torchester station on a certain day in the approaching June. Had Sir Stephen ever seriously contemplated the actual arrival of these unwelcome relations, he would certainly have been more guarded in his expressions of hospitable intent. Now, as the telegram told however, they had set foot on English soil, and no alternative

was left to the baronet but to meet his
self-exiled brother as pleasantly as possible.
The prospect was in no sense an agreeable one.   Indeed, Sir Stephen mentally
shuddered as it so closely confronted him.
He had exposed himself to receive and
to entertain these strangers for an indefi-
nite period perhaps, who certainly could
have nothing in common with him personally; nor with any of the county people
who were his usual associates.   The
habits, manners, and customs of these
quasi savages would be utterly distasteful
to him, of course.   They would offend
against his rigid notions of decorum every
hour.   Hubert had always been utterly
regardless of appearances in the old days,
and the unsettled manner of life he had
led was not likely to have improved him
in any way.   He never could be brought

to pay that deference to the small proprieties of daily life, which to Sir Stephen had become as precious as religious observances. If he was a harum-scarum fellow when he lived with gentlemen in a refined home, what would he be now after associating for years with those rebels against the social code yclept artists?

Sir Stephen was absolutely horror-struck as he contemplated the proximate invasion of his stately home by these ill-mannered *savages*. They would probably expect to dine at mid-day, and would regard the choice evening repast by which the master of Pineridge set great store as—supper.

Atrocious! And they would have disgusting German notions anent the preparation of those dishes for which the baronet's *cuisine* was justly famed throughout the county. They would add sugar to their cutlets perhaps, and vinegar to bread sauce. The dinner-hour, which was wont to be a very welcome one in the baronet's monotonous life, was now likely to turn into a social martyrdom, and the presence of a lady at his table, which ordinarily afforded pleasure to the courtly Sir Stephen, was now anticipated with misgivings akin to dread. For what manner of person was Mrs. Hubert likely to be?

An English woman by birth, yes; and the daughter of an officer; but then she had probably spent the greater part of her life in Germany, and the fact of her accepting so uncouth a husband as Hubert spoke little in favour of her refinement, according to Sir Stephen's views. At best she would turn out an unpresentable *haus frau,* having foreign predilections for *sauer-kraut* and black bread, and addicted to the frequent exercise of domestic and even menial occupations. These were favourite pursuits among the female Teutons, and they actually prided themselves on rivalling their cooks. *Mirabile dictu!* Would Mrs. Hubert think it a part of her duty to go down into the kitchen, to interfere with the maids, and, perhaps, even to dictate to the formidable Mrs. Ruskett herself?

Mrs. Ruskett was housekeeper at Pineridge, and, having managed matters entirely to her own satisfaction for many years past, was little likely to brook any interference with her prerogatives now. She, at all events, would be quite able to hold her own, thought Sir Stephen, with a deprecating shrug of his shoulders. The question was whether he should succeed as well *vis-à-vis* with this strange sister-in-law of his.

And how about the ladies in the neighbourhood—the wives and daughters of his friends? They would be sure to call upon this Mrs. Hubert. Women are always so meddlesome and inquisitive—what sort of impression would the strangers make upon them? A faint perspiration broke out on the high white forehead of the aristocratic master of Pineridge as he conjured up these terrors in his well-regulated mind, and then he bethought himself of Hubert's daughter Lina, an unkempt little brat, no doubt, as German in her manners as her name sounded. How old was she now? About four years younger than Philip, and he was just fourteen. They would be playfellows, these cousins!

At the remembrance of this relationship, Sir Stephen came to a sort of halt in his dreary reflections. It was quite distressing to think that this little foreigner, child of an unknown mother, could claim blood relationship with the sole heir of the Northcrofts. Perhaps this girl might turn out a very doubtful associate for the lad. But then, alas! nothing mattered much where helpless, useless Philip was concerned. His keen dislike to society, and inability to join in its ordinary pursuits, always kept him entirely in the background.

Such was the tenor of Sir Stephen's perplexing thoughts as he realized the now approaching consequences of his ill-considered offers at hospitality. His brother's telegram had been handed to him in his dressing-room, and he had to make quite an effort to conceal the agitation with which the sudden announcement had filled him. It had taken away all appetite for his breakfast ; and, as he entered the oak-panelled morning-room in which it was laid, he was still too pre-occupied by the contents of the pink paper he carried in his hand to heed or reply to the gentle " Good-morning, father," which came from the occupant of a chair at the further end of the table.

There was a slight acceleration in Sir Stephen's long, slow steps, and perhaps there was a degree less steadiness in the measured footfall ; for, after a moment's attentive pause, Philip, who had been listening anxiously, asked—

" Are you not well, father, or are you troubled ? "

This gentle inquiry immediately recalled the baronet to himself, and with a peremptory movement, which seemed to indicate displeasure, he answered, "Don't talk nonsense, Philip. I wish you would not give way to such ridiculous fancies. Of course I am quite well, and there is nothing whatever the matter."

Philip was silenced, but not convinced; and the stress his father laid upon his last words confirmed the sensitive lad's previous impression.

Sir Stephen then rang the bell for prayers; and while the servants, led by imposing Mrs. Ruskett the housekeeper, assemble in due form, a few words about the head of this well-organized household and his son, may not be out of place.

Sir Stephen's marriage, like most of the actions of his decorous life, was an affair of keen reflection and ample consideration. His bride elect was an only child, heiress to an old and wealthy landowner, and herself by no means in the first flush of youth. Aware that the head of the house of Northcroft had married her chiefly with a view to perpetuating the time-honoured noble name, Lady North-croft soon began to fret at the non-fulfil-ment of her grave husband's hopes, and he did not scruple to reproach her for the chagrin this disappointment caused him. Proportionately great was the joy mani-fested at Pineridge when, after some years of weary waiting and ceaseless disappointment, Lady Northcroft dis-covered that there was at last a chance of her presenting Sir Stephen with an heir, and greater still was the rejoicing with which a son was welcomed in the " an-cestral halls of his fathers"—(this was Sir Stephen's favourite formula). But, alas! his arrogant satisfaction was but of short duration; for Nature resented the cares of maternity which came so late in life upon Lady Northcroft, who only survived the birth of her boy a few weeks, and was fortunately saved from hearing the terrible doubt whispered by the nurse and doctors as to her little one's eyesight. The best skill that London could afford was sought to bring the light of science and experience to bear upon those sightless orbs. Many experiments were made, many hard names were pronounced in diagnosing the disorder, but the result was ever the same. The child's sight was failing him already, and in course of time he was doomed to be blind.

This verdict plunged the unhappy widower into the depths of despondency, and, in addition to his ordinarily morose

F 2

qualities, he now exhited a futile but bitter resentment, the brunt of which fell upon the luckless boy who was its innocent cause. For a time proud Sir Stephen refused to believe that he, the head of the house of Northcroft, could be subjected to so cruel a subversion of all the laws which govern existence; and when the fact was brought home to him by the vacant staring of those wide-open sightless baby eyes, he still thought that money—omnipotent money—could surely exempt so wealthy a man as himself from the afflictions to which less distinguished mortals are liable; and he was fairly astounded (as well he might be) that in the nineteenth century the resources of science were powerless when brought face to face with this particular form of the grave affliction of blindness.

Sir Stephen's secret but growing resentment at the mysterious ordinations of Providence unfortunately merged into cold
indifference towards his unlucky son. He
soon taught himself to regard the blind
boy as a nonentity, and at times seemed
scarcely aware of his existence. It was
unnatural, and pitiable at the same time,
to note the cruel indifference which Sir
Sir Stephen showed to the child who so
patiently endured a lasting loss which
nothing could replace, and which would
surely have entitled him to universal compassion and the sympathy of all his fellow-
creatures. But the child's affliction hardened the father's heart instead of soften-
ing it. He was too dignified, and far too
courteous a person to manifest the resentment slumbering within him by any outward harshness of speech or manner. The

owner of Pineridge was always too much
on his guard to speak harshly, and would
as soon have thought of getting into a
third-class railway carriage as into a passion. He contented himself with evinc-
ing his disgust passively only, but
often and often he wished that the
boy lay buried beside his mother, and
wished it with a concentrated passion that
would have amazed himself had he realised
its intensity. If Philip were dead his
father would be free to wed again, and
then a son after his own heart might be
born to him. But neither words nor wishes
kill, and Philip, having been tenderly
nursed during his infancy by a healthy
foster-mother, grew stronger year by year;
and, while Philip was alive, he, and he
only, could be the heir to the baronetcy.

*   *   *   *   *

Sir Stephen stands prepared now to read prayers to the domestic circle, who have gathered around him in so quiet and orderly a fashion. The bright morning sunshine, which streams straight into the room, throws his tall, well set-up figure into strong relief against the background of dark oak-panelling. The lines of his face are as hard and firm as those of his form, and neither relenting nor yielding seem possible to either. His features resemble those of Hubert, but are cut clearer, and with more decision, and he is like his plastic brother in no other respect. He wears no beard, for he belongs to the old school, which deems a moustache foppish, and condemns a beard as the sign of a ruffian. He cultivates the precisely cut mutton-chop whisker, however, as emblematic of the

English gentleman, and he has never discarded the high-collared coat and satin stock, which dates back to the Regency of " the First Gentleman in Europe."

Serious of aspect, unbending in manner, the master of Pineridge receives the Family Bible and Prayer Book from the hands of Mrs. Ruskett, the housekeeper, and he reads the comforting words of the simple service in a hard mechanical voice that robs them of half the thrilling meaning they are intended to convey to those "who have ears to hear."

Has the true import of such words as " Yea, like as a father pitieth his children even so is the Lord merciful unto them that fear Him," which he has been reading, ever occurred to this cold, cruel man ?

Prayers over, Sir Stephen makes but a

poor pretence at breakfasting. He is alone with his blind son; but he does not neglect to make a clatter with knife, fork, and spoon, in order to deceive the lad, who has reminded him of the acuteness of his hearing by the pertinent inquiry with which he received his father this morning. Philip shall not be allowed to suspect the agitation which possesses the dignified head of the house, who rather overdoes that clatter and rattling, and who, when he does speak, uses a louder tone than usual. This raising of the voice, when addressing blind persons, is a mistake constantly made by the unsympathetic, as well as the vulgar, who seem to think that loss of sight is accompanied by loss of hearing also. Philip's father, who neither understood nor compassionated the affliction of the blind boy,

certainly did all that most jarred upon
his sensitive feelings this morning. Ordinarily reserved and taciturn, he now
sought to cover his perturbation by loud
and lengthy speeches, delivered in much
the same style as those he addressed to
the prisoners brought before him in his
magisterial capacity. Philip, whose instincts (by the law of compensation) are
unusually keen, is by no means deceived
by his father's exaggerated attempts to
appear at his ease, and sits lost in silent
wonder as to what all this covert excitement portends. He is not left long in doubt.

"You will be surprised to hear that
your uncle Hubert is coming to see us
at last," says Sir Stephen, breaking a
prolonged silence with this jerky announcement. "I have read you extracts from
the *Chronicle* occasionally, as you no doubt

remember, extracts about—about his pictures—you know. He is a painter by profession (deprecatingly), but he has had an enormous success, and that reconciles me to the fact of his being an artist."

Philip vaguely wonders if artists, as a race, differ from other men and deserve contempt as a class. He knows very little of men or their pursuits, poor lad; for no one has ever taken the trouble to teach him the general facts of life. To his rustic nurse, the fostermother who saved his life as a baby, he owes such knowledge of the people and things about him as helps him to struggle through daily life with his crook-handled stick. His father's peremptory tone encourages no questions this morning, and Philip therefore resigns himself to wait for any further information that may be forthcoming.

"My brother Hubert and I have not met for many years," resumes Sir Stephen, after another thoughtful pause, "and you may imagine the gratification his advent will cause me. He will arrive with his wife and daughter this afternoon, and of course we shall all dine together at eight o'clock. I thought I would tell you the news in order that you might be prepared."

Having delivered himself of this weighty piece of information, Sir Stephen rises from the table, and pulling his chair over to the open window, he establishes himself there, unfolding his newspaper with considerable rustling, to impress upon Philip that he is reading, and does not wish to be disturbed.

The poor blind boy stifles a sigh and resigns himself to circumstances, which in this case mean *hunger*. The breakfast methodically prepared for him by the butler, who emulates his master in the austere gravity of his demeanour, has not sufficed to stay the cravings of the growing lad's hearty appetite. His father has offered him nothing, and has just intimated that he does not wish to be asked for anything either. Philip now uses his long delicate fingers, hoping to find some further provision within his reach. His hands have never been browned or hardened by handling an oar or a bat, but their gentle, sensitive touch often stands him in very good stead.

He now feels about his empty plate in vain, and without putting his cup to his lips he knows as he poises it on his fingertips that it will not yield another drop of tea. And he is so thirsty!

He leans his head on one side, listening
eagerly for any sympathetic crackle of
that engrossing newspaper; but there is
not a sound. His father is still intent
on the news, and must not be asked to
lend a helping hand as yet. Disappointed,
Philip again tries to place his hands on
the toast-rack or milk-jug, but failing to
find anything more satisfactory than a
loaf and a sardine tin, he rises, and
guiding himself carefully by the edge of
the table, he finds the corner in which
his crook-stick is resting, and eagerly
seizes this guiding friend.

A bright ray of sunshine gilds his
waving chestnut hair as he crosses the
window, and brings the golden gleams
hidden in its brown shadows to light. He
is but a stripling as yet, slim and lithe;
his well-knit frame, and long hands and

feet, give promise of height, however,
and the bright colour in his pretty young
face speaks of sound health. He presents
an amazing contrast to his hard-looking,
austere father; for the lad's appearance is
gentle, almost to girlishness, and the unusual length of his hair, which no one
seems to think of cutting for him, adds to
this impression. In watching him as he
cautiously moves along in blind helplessness a feeling of intense compassion would
possess most beholders, but to his father
he is an eyesore only, and the servants
in the house, taking their cue from the
master, treat his poor son with scant
courtesy and very little consideration. It
is the general immobility of the lad's face
which suggests his blindness; not the eyes
themselves, for they are wide open, and
bear no outward sign of the cruel infir-

mity which has rendered them useless. As he reaches the door of the breakfast-room, Philip turns towards the window once again, and listens wistfully for some detaining word or sign. But his father is still absorbed in that interesting news-paper, and the boy leaves the august presence with less notice than a dog might receive.

CHAPTER V.

WHEN once the journey to England was definitely settled on, it became the all-absorbing topic of conversation in the happy little artistic home in Munich. Lina was to leave the German day-school she had regularly attended for the last four years, and would henceforth be taught entirely by her devoted mother. This was a task the latter undertook very gladly, as the child's English had been somewhat neglected. This had been a matter of regret to ·Mrs. Northcroft, and she was pleased to think that under her own tuition this great need in her child's education would be

rectified. The lessons were commenced
with additional zeal now that a visit to
England was in prospect; for Lina was
most anxious to meet her new cousin on
equal terms. About this cousin the
child asked about a thousand questions.
Father had told her that Philip was
blind.

Blind! What did that sad sounding
word, so gravely spoken, really mean?
It was blind in English, and *blind* in
German; but the sound conveyed no
definite impression to the anxiously-
inquiring Lina. Wondering, and seriously perplexed, the child consulted her
mother on the subject so entirely preoccupying her. And Mrs. Northcroft,
with patient seriousness, explained the
sad nature of Philip's affliction.

Full of sorrow, and keenly sympathetic,

the little girl resolved on teaching herself practically what she found it so
difficult to realize from the descriptions
given her. She tied a handkerchief over
her eyes, and thus blindfolded she felt
her way about the rooms, stumbling
often on her experimental journey.
Once she tried to dress her doll with
the bandage over her eyes; but finding
herself quite at a loss, she jumped up
in a state of mind bordering on despair,
and flinging the toy on one side, refused
to play or to be pacified. "It is dreadful, too dreadful," she cried. On another
occasion she endeavoured to eat her
dinner with her eyes closed; but she
suddenly burst into a flood of tears, and,
sobbing, exclaimed, "Oh, my poor darling cousin Philip, how unhappy you
must be.

After this final and convincing experiment Lina tried no others. The sad reality had come home to her with a grievous shock ; the child's sensitive nature suffered under it. Her next absorbing idea was to find out how she would best be able to help her cousin, and with this end in view she studied English, reading so diligently that before she left Munich she could manage to read, page after page, of any easy book fluently and with little or no foreign accent.

"And how can *he* do his lessons, mother?" she asked one day : "Should I be able to teach and help him with them?"

Mrs. Northcroft explained the mystery of the embossed letters, &c., and subsequently took her daughter to the blind

school, where she beheld the practical
teaching of the afflicted ones, and
wondered greatly at their skill, and at
the cheerful way in which they spoke.
" Do you think Philip will be happy,
and laugh as they do, mother?" she
asked, wistfully, and mentally resolved to
do all she possibly could to please and
amuse that poor dear cousin, who could
not see the bright sunshine, the birds,
the trees and flowers, nor even the
faces of those about him.

When the actual preparations for the
long and anxiously anticipated journey
were commenced in right earnest, Lina
had less time to ponder on the all-
engrossing subject of her afflicted cousin ;
and the child's high spirits and natural
vivacity caused her to find endless
amusement in the trouble and discomfort

attendant upon the break up of a home.
It had been settled by Hubert (who on
this occasion displayed unwonted energy
and decision) that the studio and " flat "
in the old house in Munich should be
let to an artist and his family for one
year certain. Hubert had actually made
up his mind to reside in England for
twelve months at least; if not with his
brother, at any rate in some separate
establishment. At the end of that time
he would be in a better position, no doubt,
to arrive at a further decision. Mrs.
Hubert, who never opposed her husband
when she found him resolved on a point,
yielded, as usual, though with inordinate
misgivings. But she wisely refrained
from obtruding these upon her easy-
going lord, and as he was more than
usually occupied just now in finishing a

pet picture, which he was bound to deliver within a certain time, she had the more leisure to devote to little Lina, whose marked intelligence and sensitive temperament were a source of lasting pleasure and interest to the high-minded, simple-hearted mother. She influenced Lina's every thought, and fostered the child's natural spirit of unselfishness with tenderest care. She never repressed the exuberance of Lina's child-like gaiety; nor did she check the high spirits which made her a very sunshine in her present home. Hubert, who was of a calm, equable temper, as we know, was not likely to display much emotion as the time for migration arrived; but though outwardly quiet and indifferent, as usual, he was in reality more perturbed than he cared to let his wife know. A variety of novel sensations were at work within him, and he scarcely knew himself whether he was most glad or sorry at the thought of revisiting the home of his boyhood.

By the time the family party was fairly *en route*, he, who was never very talkative, lapsed into a silence that in another man would have seemed sullen. And the placidity which was his chief characteristic disappeared altogether as soon as he set foot on English soil. His wife noted these odd changes of mood in her calm and hitherto unimpressionable lord; but she was too wise a woman to trouble him about them. She knew if she left him "to work his way round" unmolested, he would the sooner return to his normal condition of cheerful content, and she gladly resigned herself to bide her time. Meanwhile she really had little leisure to think about her husband's vagaries; for Lina's eager excitement grew with every passing hour. It was with the greatest difficulty, and only " to please dear mother," that the child could be made to sit still. In the train, on the steamer, and also in the carriage that met the party at Torchester station, her constant impulse appeared to be to jump out of the window, and run to the goal of the long tiresome journey.

Pineridge Priory is pleasantly situate in that part of Torshire where the trees from which it takes its name abound. And as the carriage enters the outer gate of the plantation which leads on to the home park, Mrs. Hubert realizes the accuracy of the descriptions her husband has so often given her of his old home.

" Oh, pine trees ! Christmas trees ! " cries Lina, inhaling the luscious scent of the plantation through which they were driving. "There is no smell I like better than that. It is so sweet and so strong too, and it makes me remember. . . . ."

The bright childish face is lifted, the delicate nostrils inhale the grateful perfume with delight, and into the large thoughtful eyes there comes a longing, dreamy look—a look so full of tender recollections as to be almost sorrowful. She says, " *Tannenbaum !* " as German children utter the magic word which is so pregnant of Christmas delight to them. Her life among the fair-haired Teutons seems to have made her one of them. Instead of responding to her delighted exclamations with cheerful encouragement, Hubert, who is decidedly "odd" to-day, shakes his head and frowns.

"Tut, tut, tut!" he says, in what sounds almost like reproof, "Don't be so romantic, Lina, and pray don't talk nonsense. We have come into a land of prose and matter of fact, where my pictures and your reminiscences will not be appreciated at all." He laughs, but the laugh is a forced one, and sensible Lina feeling herself rebuked, becomes silent.

Mrs. Northcroft glances uneasily from father to child, and again a shade of anxiety clouds her frank, handsome face. Hubert perceiving it, takes an extra long whiff from the pipe he has just lighted. "Hugh, dearest," says his wife, entreatingly, "pray put your pipe out of sight. We shall be at the house in a minute,

and you really must show a little consideration for your brother's prejudices.
What will he think if you arrive smoking
in that way? In Rome you must do
as Rome does, surely. What is accepted
in Germany may, perhaps, seem atrocious
here."

She speaks with the utmost gentleness,
but Hubert does not like the implied
reproof. He shrugs his shoulders im-
patiently, and his sigh is decidedly petu-
lant. He adopts his wife's suggestion
nevertheless; and having knocked the
glowing tobacco out of the obnoxious
pipe, he endeavours to hide it in the
breast-pocket of his coat. But the stem
which is long, persists in protruding, and
it is Lina's ready little hand which carefully hides it under the broad collar of
the brown velveteen garment. Mrs. Hu-

bert is now becoming nervous in her turn. She cannot conquer a certain dread of the consequences of the meeting between brothers so long estranged. Personally she has no pleasure in the idea of spending weeks—months, perhaps, under the roof of prim, prejudiced Sir Stephen; but now as ever, her husband's will is law to her, and she is determined to do all she can to add to the harmony of the meeting. When the brothers come to know one another better, all is sure to go well. The overbearing spirit of the elder, the wild impulse and passionate action of the younger, are all matters of the past now, and the present will surely be productive of that kind and cheerful intercourse which Letitia, who is a true, loving woman, deems essential to the well-being of those about her. She is quick-sighted too, this clever wife of Hubert's, and fully aware of the value of first impressions. Therefore she is doubly anxious that a good one shall be made now.

Sir Stephen hears the carriage wheels upon the gravel drive, with an amount of trepidation that dismays him. He calls himself an idiot in the faintest of whispers, and mastering his agitation by a strong effort, he leaves his library with a feeling akin to sickness which makes his pale face livid. "Courteous" he must ever be, that is his creed, and it demands that he shall receive these unwelcome guests with every outward show of hospitality.

He meets them on the threshold, and so accurately times his movements that he holds out welcoming hands just as Hubert and his wife pass in between the footmen, who open the wings of the old-fashioned oak door. Mr. Grind, the butler, is at his master's back, and the whole ceremony is made as imposing as possible. Mrs. Ruskett, from a distant point of observation, is also taking stock of the strangers, whom she angrily dubs " intruders," and a crimson flush dyes her round face as she comes to the conclusion that Mrs. Hubert North-croft is a *lady*.

" Leastwise she behaves herself as such."

This is the housekeeper's confidential verdict, whispered to austere Mr. Grind later in the evening.

The first glance at his brother convinces Sir Stephen that, beyond looking older, Hubert is Hubert still, to all intents and purposes, unchanged. But the baronet is agreeably surprised to find that his sister-in-law is an elegant, lady-like woman, who wears her simple but well-made travelling dress with grace, and bears herself as though quite accustomed to the honour of shaking hands with a county magnate. His quietly observant eye falls on the child too, and he is struck by the bright beauty of the intelligent little face, though the slight trace of a German accent somewhat jars upon his sensitive ear.

They all stand at the foot of the broad oak staircase unconsciously absorbed in taking stock of one another, while they utter vague remarks upon the length of the journey, the beauty of the weather, the country, etc., etc.

Suddenly, with a cry of pity and alarm, Lina darts from Sir Stephen's side, and before any one has ascertained the cause of her distress, she is bounding up the stairs two steps at a time, to where Philip, with slow caution, is commencing his descent.

He holds the balustrade with one hand and his crook-stick in the other.

" Oh ! let me guide you ; pray, let me help you ; mind you don't fall," cries the eager little maid, and she lays her caress-ing hand on his arm with the utmost tenderness. " You are my dear, dear cousin," she whispers close to his ear, " and I am going to stay with you and help you in everything, just as much as ever I can. Mother has told me many things I can do for you, and you will always let me try to be useful to you, won't you? "

Poor Philip stands quite still ; he is first startled, then amazed. The sweet, strange childish voice close to his ear, the gentle pressure of those tiny fingers on his, and above all, the electric sympathy which thrills him as he becomes conscious of her loving presence; all these new sensations bewilder him. He stands waiting irresolute. He is dazzled, poor lad, by the first sunny ray of the love which lights up the double darkness of his sad young life; but it soon produces a delicious sense of warmth and animation within him, and he clasps that soft tiny hand closely, firmly with his long supple fingers.

"I shall be so glad and so thankful if you will help me a little, my *dear* cousin," he says eagerly, and, as he speaks, a flush of shyness steals slowly up into his pretty, refined face.

"He looks like a sorry angel," she tells her mother, by-and-by. Meanwhile she leads him gently, step by step, down to the lofty hall, where his kind-hearted uncle clasps him fondly in his arms. Philip feels that this is a day of glorious revelation for him, and that such happiness may be in store for him yet, as he, with his sightless eyes, could never have ventured to anticipate.

CHAPTER VI

FIRST IMPRESSIONS.

THE Master of Pineridge, a little impatient of the demonstrative greetings bestowed upon his son, leads Mrs. Northcroft into the library, and the rest of the party follow. Presently a gong sounds.

"We dine in half an hour," says Sir Stephen; "so I suppose we must separate for a time. Grind will wait upon you, Hubert, and Mrs. Ruskett has told off a maid to attend to the ladies. Shall we adjourn?"

"You are not expecting any guests to-night, are you, Stephen?" asks Hubert, with evident anxiety.

"Guests? No. Is there any one you desire to meet?" Stephen speaks in a tone of protest, as though accused of neglecting a duty.

"Not in the least, my dear boy; not in the least," answers Hubert, with a sigh of relief; "and that being so," he adds eagerly, "there will be no occasion for me to dress, eh?"

"Do just as you please, brother, just as you please," says the host; but, though his words are amiable, his tone is by no means encouraging—there is a ring of cold displeasure in it which does not escape the quick ear of Letitia.

"If you dress, Hubert will do the same," she says, glancing at Sir Stephen and bowing her pretty head.

"I invariably dress for dinner," he says in his most pompous tone. "With me it is a matter not of inclination, but of principle. A change is requisite after a day's exercise, and it is the right thing to do. It is impossible to keep up the dignity of your position if you do not impress your servants. If you make it a rule to dress for dinner, your valet is kept up to the mark, and you reduce your butler to his proper level. If you neglect appearances the man who waits upon you is apt to look down upon you in every sense. But pray do not let my rules interfere with your convenience, Hubert. Do just as you please, I beg of you."

"He might have spared us that oration," the artist mutters below his breath, and turns appealingly to his wife.

"You are afraid you cannot lay your hand upon your dress clothes, dear," she says, with her pleasant smile; "but I can unpack them for you in two minutes. I know exactly how they were stowed away. Come, let us make haste." She puts her hand on his arm, and so compels him to leave the room with her.

"What a confounded nuisance!" he mutters, as soon as the door is closed behind them. "This is the sort of penance expected and dreaded all along. Stephen is just the same stilted prig as ever. He preaches about manners and morals *ad nauseam*, and he practises——"

"Hush, Hugh, hush, dearest," whispers his wife in a tone of entreaty.

"Well, it is disagreeable, deuced disagreeable," says he, by no means pacified. "I have not had a dress coat on for months and months. The livery of society! Ugh! I hate society, its liveries, and the rest of its shams. The idea of wearing a coat that has not even a pocket for one's pipe in it! If Stephen chooses to dress and to be a humbug, let him; but why should I be bothered? I shall pretty soon get tired of him and all his dignity, I know. I'm sorry I came; and I most certainly shall not stand this sort of thing very long."

"Nonsense, my dear old grumbler," says his wife, cheerily; "your vexation is actually making you eloquent. I have not heard so lengthy a speech from you since——"

"Since I proposed the health of our dear old Reuter at that jolly festival of artists; eh, Letty? Yes, I certainly did make a good speech that day."

"A splendid speech!" she replies, gaily. She has diverted his thoughts from a disagreeable topic, and she has succeeded in laying all the things needful for his toilette, ready to his hand.

When Mr. Grind knocks at the door of the dressing-room to offer his services, he is considerably startled to find that "artiss chap" looking as much like a gentleman as his own dignified master does.

Before descending Hubert presents himself at the door of his wife's room for inspection and approval.

"If it were not for a whiff of something rather like smoke you would be perfect, my dear," she says, smiling, and begins to sprinkle some lavender water on his coat, while she adds: "Dare I paraphrase Moore for your benefit, and suggest:

"'You may wash, you may comb the beard as you will; But the scent of tobacco, it lingers there still'?"

Hubert is always docile under his wife's management, and her sweet temper and ready wit have driven all storm-clouds from the domestic horizon as usual. He himself is amazed at his personal transformation, of which he becomes suddenly aware, as he enters the drawing-room, and beholds a good-looking, well-groomed Hubert in the long glass which faces the door.

"I had no idea I was such a presentable fellow," he whispers to Letitia, and she nods smilingly in confirmation. Hubert feels a little disappointed to find that Sir Stephen forbears to make any comment on the favourable change in his appearance. The host is agreeably impressed by the concession his brother has made to the customs of the house; but he is far too dignified to remark on the transformation. Personal comments in any case show a want of breeding, and familiarity, even towards a brother, would have been detrimental to that stately courtesy on which Sir Stephen especially prides himself.

"Philip usually dines in the middle of the day," says the host, in answer to an anxious question from little Lina, "but to-night he shall join us, as you will be with us also, and his cover shall be laid beside yours, as you wish."

"Thank you, *dear* uncle," cries the child eagerly, and she put up her rosy face for a kiss. She is the only one of the party who is not overawed by the oppressive dignity of the host ; indeed, she is far too much engrossed in watching and attending upon her cousin to spare a thought for herself or any one else. But that evening, when she had said her prayers, and Mrs. Northcroft bent over to give her the last good-night kiss, the child whispered the impression her new relations had made on her. " Uncle Stephen is a grand, fine gentleman," said this acute observer, " but he is a little too proud of himself. Don't you think so, mother?"

"And what do you think of your poor cousin?" asks Mrs. Northcroft, smiling.

"Oh! Philip is a darling."

Hubert, who sits opposite the children at dinner-time, watches them with a smile of happy content upon his pleasant face.

"That's right, Lina, take care of your cousin," he says approvingly. "Arrange his plate like the face of a clock, cut everything up very small, put the meat at six, the potatoes at twelve, and the peas at nine. There, that's capital! Now, Phil, you will very soon find your way."

"Nurse taught me the clock face," whispers Philip, shyly, to Lina.

He lives in constant dread of a sharp silencing word from his father But the baronet makes no audible sign of disapproval, though he raises his eyebrows and curls his lips. These random suggestions of Hubert to the blind boy sound like nonsense to the unsympathetic parent, who is quite unable to appreciate the practical value of his brother's remarks. But to Lina and Philip both those lightly spoken words present a feasible hint, and the clever, observant little maid arranges the viands on her cousin's plate as if it were the face of the clock as her father has proposed. Then she guides the hand that holds the fork, and points successively to meat, potatoes and peas. Philip endeavours, with the quick sensitiveness of touch and apprehension which are given as a merciful compensation for the sad absence of sight, to seize on his uncle's suggestion as still another of those wondrous revelations with which this strange and delightful day seems fraught. And so useful is the simple method indicated, that the blind boy, with his cousin's kind assistance, easily finds out and distinguishes the various contents of his plate, instead of floundering hopelessly with his knife and fork among the unsorted food. He presently begins to eat his dinner with nearly as much facility as though he can see what he is doing, and as they rise from the ceremonious feast, to which the presence of the children has given its sole redeeming feature, Philip glides his hand gently under Hubert's arm, and whispers gratefully—

"Thank you so much, my dear uncle. I shall know how to manage my meals much better now, and I shall think of you whenever I have my dinner." Then, led by Lina, he follows his aunt into the drawing-room, and the brothers are left to their port and their confidences.

Mrs. Northcroft is tired, and seats herself in a lounging-chair by the window that opens on to the broad stone terrace. She is content to rest now, for the ordeal of the first stately dinner is over, and has been passed satisfactorily. This bodes well for the future peace of the establishment, and Hubert's wife is thankful for his dear sake.

"Do let us go out into the garden," says Lina, placing her hand on Philip's arm, "and pick some flowers for mother while she is resting. She loves roses, and so do I." The cousin assents, and they wander forth together out of the

open window, across the terrace, and
down the broad flight of steps that leads
to the well-kept paths of the flower
garden.

"Will you sit here and wait for me
while I get the roses?" says Lina. And
she establishes Philip on a bench. Having
gathered a bunch of early roses, Lina
looks across at the blind boy, and stands
still, eagerly watching him. He has re-
lapsed into his usual attitude, which is
one of profound melancholy. It is only
when he is spoken to or interested that
he rouses himself. Now his chin has sunk
upon his breast, his hands hang listlessly
by his side. Lina is transfixed by an
impulse of intense pity, of overwhelming
tenderness. Tears fill her eyes. Oh!
would that she might give him the sight
she has never valued until now! Poor,

sad, and much-to-be-pitied Philip! How good, how very, very patient and good she must be to him always—always. How hard she will strive to brighten his dreary days!

"I am coming, cousin," she cries, brushing her tears away, and making an effort to speak gaily. She is immediately rewarded. A smile, so sweet and bright as to gladden her heart thoroughly, is his response, as he rises, stick in hand, and guides himself to meet her, following the sound of her gentle voice.

She lays her hands on his shoulders when she meets him, and, putting her sweet child's face up to his, kisses his lips.

" I want to promise you, cousin Philip, to promise you faithfully, dear, that I will always love you, and always be good to you, if I can. I want to take care of you and help you, more than I want anything else in all the wide world."

Thus earnestly, solemnly, the child Lina sets her seal to the bond between them, which in the time to come holds her through storm and trouble, through misfortune and trial, steadfast, devoted, and true.

The impulse in the child's heart, though it throbs on earth, is prompted by a spirit Divine, for it is dictated by a pure and perfect love.

*   *   *   *   *

A great sense of peace and content steals into the hearts of the children as they walk onward, hand in hand. They are silent, but their hearts are full to overflowing ; tears stand in Lina's eyes, tears of a holy and infinite compassion, and two glittering drops roll slowly over Philip's cheeks. His heart is melted within him. The dawn of a new life of bright and beautiful days seems to him to be beginning with this sunset hour— the hour in which words of devotion, of precious promise, have been spoken to him, the hour in which gentle hands have guided him cautiously, and the sweet pressure of a small child's lips upon his own has revealed the first glimpse of a new and wonderful world to him—the bright world of love.

"Let us go back to mother, and ask her to play us soft music," says Lina, at last. The prolonged silence is becoming painful to her. She has no clue as yet to her companion's thoughts, and whenever he is silent she fears he is unhappy. Music is always soothing and delightful. Philip surely loves music too, and mother plays so sweetly!

When the children return to the drawing room, they find the gentlemen there. Lina lays her roses on her mother's lap, and makes her petition, "Philip would like it so much," she says, "and you and I will teach him to play; won't we, mother?"

The fine old Broadwood, that has scarcely been used since Lady Northcroft's death, is readily opened by Hubert for his wife, and the baronet looks on at all these innovations with considerable surprise, but without any protest. In truth he finds his brother's wife admirable and is not inclined to quarrel with anything she does. And she plays exceedingly well. She abstains altogether from musical fireworks, but her touch is exquisite, and she renders some lovely melodies with a grace and purity which even Sir Stephen appreciates, and which lead him to signify his approval.

Philip sits perfectly silent, far away in a corner by the window. It is only when Lina, in obedience to her mother's behest, begins to sing that he creeps slowly, cautiously across the room, until he stands by her side. She sings in a clear, childish treble, and the ditties she has learnt are simple German *volkslieder;* but to Philip it seems as if heaven has opened, and her voice is the voice of an angel.

"How happy you are all making me to-day!" he whispers to his uncle, as he bids him good-night. "I have thought it very hard to be blind at times, but I shall never think so again if you will all stay here and make life glad and bright for us."

"Will you come down at six and walk in the garden with me, cousin?" asks Lina, as she turns to follow Mrs. Northcroft out of the room. "It is so beautiful out of doors in the early morning."

"I shall not sleep at all, for fear of being later than you are," says he, smiling; and thoroughly satisfied, they all take leave of one another for the the night.

CHAPTER VII

UNDER-CURRENTS.

THE first few hours of his intercourse with his newly arrived relatives were sufficient to lift a great weight from Sir Stephen's mind, and to relieve him of the growing anxieties which he had spent the last day or two in conjuring up to his own torment. Like many imaginary evils, these disappeared the moment they were confronted in the flesh, and his first interview with his relatives over, Sir Stephen breathed freely again. Hubert was certainly still the same easy-going pipe-smoking Hubert as of yore; but even he was improved in many respects. Matrimony had certainly

had a highly beneficial influence upon
him. It was evident that he was ready
to submit with a good grace to the
practical suggestions of his discreet wife,
and though himself as regardless of *les
convenances* as of yore, he obeyed her
well-timed directions without much protest. As to Mrs. Hubert herself, Sir
Stephen was fairly amazed, and pondered
with increasing surprise on the startling
fact that so refined and well-bred a lady
should have condescended to marry so
harum-scarum an individual as his artist
brother. The owner of Pineridge felt
almost inclined to pity his sister-in-law;
but as she was evidently quite content
with her lot, and very much attached to
her erratic husband, compassion was out
of place: a shrug of the shoulders, a
curl of the thin lips, and a muttered

" unaccountable beings are women, " sufficed to express his astonishment.

That Lina showed signs of great promise, and was in every respect a charming counterpart of her mother, was natural. The excellent influence of the latter was already visible in all the child said and did. Sir Stephen regretted that so foreign-sounding a name had been given to his niece, and he hoped that in the course of time she would overcome the slight German accent with which she spoke her native language. But what faults he had to find were all due to Hubert's eccentricity, as he had already ascertained in questioning his brother during their first confidential post-prandial chat. Hubert had insisted on the child's having a German nurse during her infancy, and Hubert had chosen the objectionable German name, because it belonged to his first love—a dear little German maid he had met as a student, and whom he would have married, had she not died.

"And does your wife know all this romantic folly ?" asked Sir Stephen, poising his wine-glass daintily between his long slender fingers.

"My wife knows the true story of my life," answered Hubert, with a deep sigh. "She was thankful to find that so heedless a fellow as her artist husband was capable of a lasting and grateful memory. It seemed a guarantee of my constancy in the future. Letty is a very sensible— perhaps a remarkable—woman, Stephen; when you know her better, you will find out that I have had the good fortune to draw a prize in the great lottery called marriage."

"I have arrived at that comfortable conclusion already," said Sir Stephen pom-
pously. He seemed to think that his
approval put the necessary hall-mark upon
what without it would have been but a
poor imitation. Hubert hid a smile under
his beard as he responded to some further
laudatory comments on "that exceptionally
charming woman, my sister-in-law!" "He
evidently forgot that she had to be my
wife before she aspired to that honour,"
thought Hubert; but he drank his wine
in silence, and was content to know that
his Letty was appreciated at head-quarters,
even if he were still disapproved of.

Of Philip's delight at the coming of his
kind relations there could be no doubt.
So great was his happiness, poor lad, that
he really could not sleep; but, as the
thoughts crowding one after another into

his active brain were essentially pleasant ones, he rose quite refreshed in the morning, and awaited the chiming of the great hall clock, which would proclaim the hour six, with intense eagerness. There was neither dawn nor rousing morning sun for him; but a new day was shining in his heart, and he longed for a repetition of the sweet experience of that bright yesterday. He felt sure that he should find all he was seeking as soon as he was in Lina's presence again, listening to the musical sounds of her soft speech, feeling the encouraging pressure of her small guiding hand, knowing that at last he had found some one to care for—to love him, some one who thought it a pleasure to come to his aid, and who would pity rather than condemn him for his helplessness.

But there was another and a very important personage in that oddly assorted household, on whom the arrival of the Hubert Northcrofts had by no means so tranquilising an effect. This was Mrs. Sarah Ruskett, the housekeeper. On the death of her late mistress, Lady Northcroft (fourteen years ago), Mrs. Ruskett had assumed the reins of government as far as the domestic establishment at the Priory was concerned, and no one had questioned her absolute authority in the slightest degree; but the advent of Mrs. Hubert filled her suspicious soul with instant and insurmountable misgivings. Who could tell the upshot of that lady's arrival at the house of her brother-in-law? She was sure to be of the interfering inquisitive sort. And a former experience of the housekeeper warranted

her in dreading the power of female
relations where bachelors or widowers
were concerned.   They always made a
point, those " benevolent " ladies, of peer-
ing into the private affairs of their lonely
relatives, which was apt to result in all
sorts of unpleasantness.   For the devoted
housekeeper had done her very best
for the bereaved gentleman, " that she
had."

The chances were that Mrs. Hubert
would discover some flaws in Mrs.
Ruskett's domestic management ; or, at all
events, she would make a point of saying
that matters were not as they should be.
" It's always the way with those ladies
that come interfering in other people's
houses," thought anxious Mrs. Sarah,
wearily.   And then she wondered if Mrs.
Hubert would have the bad taste to con-

fide her disapproval to the master of the house, when she felt herself more at home there. She seemed to be quite at her ease with Sir Stephen already, and his high and mighty manner, which chilled most people, had evidently not had the effect of subduing that lady, or that forward little child, who seemed to have taken the most wonderful fancy to the blind boy from the first, and who showed no more fear of the haughty baronet than she did of his silly, helpless son. There was no knowing where all this wonderful friendliness and sudden intimacy might lead.

Mrs. Northcroft might actually go so far as to question the extent of the household expenditure. She might even presume to interfere in this sacred matter personally, or worse still, to suggest the

propriety of doing so to the austere
master of the Priory.

The thought of that forward Miss Lina,
was a terrible thorn in the flesh to the
greatly perturbed housekeeper. The lad
was still very young, and the girl a mere
child; but he was heir to the baronetcy,
to all his father's wealth too, and she was
evidently a *very* knowing young lady.
Perhaps she had actually been taught to
play her cards already; much as Mrs.
Ruskett had taught a similar lesson to
her own daughter, black-eyed, bouncing,
loud-spoken Miss Isabel. Was this fair-
haired, soft little cousin about to interfere in schemes so ambitious, so fraught
with exceeding importance, that Sarah
Ruskett herself hardly dared to confront
them in all the possible magnitude of
their results?

Like Iago she might have whispered—

"'Tis here; but yet confused—
Knavery's plain face is never seen till used."

That she *had* made wondrous plans for
the future of her only child was an un-
doubted fact. She was educating Isabel
up to some destiny far beyond what her
present position implied, and to further
her ambitious views, now that the girl
had turned fifteen, she had sent her to a
ladies' school at Brighton, where a heavy
fee entitled her to share the lessons of
those who socially were immeasurably her
superiors. Mrs. Ruskett was determined
that, come what might, Isabel should at
least be capable of holding her own, both
as regards manners and accomplishments,
with any real-born lady in the world.

Now the sudden and unwelcome advent
of these bothering relations of her master

seemed to act as a check on the housekeeper's covert aspirations, and she could
not subdue the fear that their visit, if
prolonged, would prove detrimental to
her Isabel, who was only about eighteen
months older than Mr. Philip.   Some
years ago this girl had been allowed to
play with him occasionally.   Sir Stephen
would not have sanctioned the constant
companionship of his son with Mrs.
Ruskett's daughter, but, under the circumstances, there was no valid objection
to her taking the place of his guide and
attendant at times.   The girl, however,
who was naturally selfish and hot-tempered,
found no pleasure in a task which, above
all else, required gentleness and patience,
and she fiercely resented her mother's
constant behest to go and look after
Master Philip.   She certainly did not add

much to the poor lad's comfort or happiness while she was a resident at Pineridge, and yet his affectionate nature and sad helplessness had taught him to cling to and depend upon her to a great extent. And when her mother despatched her to the boarding school at Brighton, Philip fretted considerably, and often lamented her absence. This parting had taken place at the end of the last Christmas holidays, just a few months before the arrival of Lina.

The only other individual who to any extent was concerned in ministering to the wants of Philip after Isabel's departure was a Mr. Blunt, who came over twice a week from the School for the Blind at Torchester. He taught young Northcroft to read by the aid of embossed letters, and otherwise educated him as far as the

schoolmaster's very limited powers permitted him to do. For the greater
portion of his long lonely days, poor
Philip was left to his own devices entirely,
and it was an optional matter with coach-
man, housekeeper, or butler to allow one
of the lower servants to take the son of
the house for his walks abroad. If their
services were required by their superior
officers, neither footman nor groom was
allowed to attend to the blind boy, and
he was far too gentle and resigned to his
hard fate to rebel openly against the
decrees issued from the housekeeper's
room.

Sir Stephen never took the slightest
trouble about his boy, beyond ostenta-
tiously leading him in and out of church
every Sunday, and this he did as if he
would say to the admiring on-lookers,

"Behold the devotion of the greatest among you to one hopelessly afflicted, who would be helpless but for this condescension!" When he and the boy were alone he scarcely rendered him any assistance whatever; but (if the butler were present) he would occasionally read scraps of news aloud from the morning papers, or in the evening would pretend to listen to a chapter from the Bible, which the blind boy was at such infinite pains to fumble out with puzzled and weary fingers on the embossed pages. Sir Stephen had come to regard his son as a useless encumbrance only, and it never occurred to the selfish, inconsiderate elder that other resources than those of field sports were available to the blind boy.

Had it been possible to send Philip to a public school, the father would have

deemed distinction in the cricket field or
with the oar far beyond any academic
success.   His ambition had been that his
son should grow up and follow in his own
footsteps.   Prowess in those sports, identi-
fied with the typical gentleman of provincial England, ranked above "book
learning" in the narrow mind of the
baronet.

It was probably the deplorable fact
that Philip was considered a nonentity at
Pineridge which first suggested an amazing scheme for his future subjection to
Mrs. Ruskett.   But, however events might
turn, a "first-class education" could not
do otherwise than redound to her own
and her daughter's credit in the years to
come.   It was on this account she had
resolved to invest a portion of her considerable savings (?) in procuring Isabel's

admission to the fashionable school of the Misses Pruce, of Adelaide Square, Brighton. Had Mrs. Ruskett foreseen the possibility of Lina's advent on the scene she would most assuredly not have sent her daughter out of the way at so critical a juncture. But that young lady was already learning to ape her betters and wear her new handsome dresses with infinite arrogance, when simple, affectionate Lina arrived at Pineridge. Meanwhile this sweet-natured child devoted herself solely to her afflicted cousin from the first hour of their meeting, and she soon became eyes, hands, and feet, to him.

The light of her love brought sunshine into his existence now, and with every passing day he felt the sorrow of his benighted state less acutely.

CHAPTER VIII.

ART PROGRESS.

HUBERT'S unquenchable love for his art revives, and begins to show itself strong as ever a very few days after his arrival at Pineridge. The characteristics of the English scenery attract and fascinate him. He wanders away into the open, sets up his easel and camp-stool, and goes to work with his usual undemonstrative enthusiasm and concentrated energy. He soon completes some happy sketches and studies of foreground and bramble, sandbank or rural road. The running brook up beyond the plantation makes a charming "bit," and especially delights admiring Lina. The baronet regards his eccentric brother's proceedings with mild deprecation. There is no harm in this mania, and it does not interfere in the least with any of Sir Stephen's farming occupations, and, as most of the county families are away in London at this time of the year, he has nothing to fear from their criticisms of his brother's undignified and trivial pursuits.

Hubert had established his reputation chiefly by the portrayal of foreign scenery, and now he was determined to prove to his admirers that he could deal with the peculiar beauties of his native land as successfully as with other subjects. His desire was to paint a notable picture in Torshire this year, which he might afterwards send or take to Munich, and thence forward to other continental exhibitions.

Philip displayed the keenest interest about this sketching and painting of which he heard his uncle talk, and asked a thousand questions of Lina on the subject. He felt all the brushes, the palette, the cleaning knife, the colour tubes, canvas and mahl-stick. The whole procedure was a subject of profound interest to him.

"You shall come out sketching with father to-day," says Lina, one morning when Hubert had just declared his intention of taking up some outdoor work. "I often went with him when we lived abroad, and now we will both go. We will sit behind him very quietly, we won't disturb him a bit, and I will tell you all he does in a whisper. That won't worry him. I will tell you all he does, and what colours he uses. When you are tired of hearing all about that—and its only the same thing over and over again, but just with a different colour now and then—I shall read you a pretty story. Mother says I can manage almost any book now. What have you heard, and what would you like best?"

"I don't know," says Philip, with a deprecating movement of head and hand. "I don't think I have ever heard any real stories."

"What! has no one ever read you Andersen's lovely Fairy Tales, or Grimm's, or the stories from Shakespeare?"

Philip listens to her eager questions in evident dejection.

"I know none of them," he says, "but I remember some one once told me I ought to hear Sir Walter Scott's novels. Have you ever read those, Lina?"

"Not all of them," she answered, pleased

to confess that she also is ignorant, since this will reconcile him to his want of information, " but I know ' Ivanhoe ' and ' The Talisman ; ' mother read them to me : they are such beautiful stories ; and I have read part of them again to myself since. I have the books, and we will take one of them out with us, and I will try and read it to you ; won't that be nice ? How very glad I am that you have never heard them ! You will like them so much, I am sure—only they are very long, and some of the words are very hard. You will not mind my being rather slow in pronouncing them, I hope, dear cousin ? "

" I shall indeed like to listen, and I will be very patient, I promise you," says Philip ; " I have never heard any story read steadily through from beginning to end yet. Martin, the groom, once began to read me a book called 'The Old English Gentleman,' but that was all about horses and dogs and farms. I did not care much about it, because I could not understand it. I begged him to read 'Robinson Crusoe' to me, and I gave him all my pocket money, for I dearly wanted to hear that story ; but he said it was rubbish, and only fit for babies. If I wanted to read that sort of stuff, he said, I had better get it in the print I could understand myself. He thought it might be done in embossed letters ; but it turned out that nothing really worth reading was ever printed in them except the Bible. It appears Mr. Blunt gave him this information when he drove him over from Torchester one morning, and Mr. Blunt has certainly never got me any book except the Bible, and oh, how often have I been thankful for that!"

Lina looks wistfully at the boy; her large, loving eyes fill with tears. The compassion she feels for him grows with each passing hour, there are moments when she feels as if she must take some instant and forcible revenge on the cruel, cruel people who have so long and so terribly neglected this patient, uncomplaining sufferer. But he shall not know that his trouble makes her cry. She brushes her tears away hastily, and clears the choking sob in her throat as she says with admirable cheerfulness—

"So much the better, Phil dear, there will be all the more for me to read to you. I can tell you 'Robinson Crusoe' right off; I have that in German and English too; you *will* like it, and we can act it! We will play at it in the garden, and fancy we are wrecked on the grass-plot. What fun we shall have! But besides our games we will do all sorts of learning too. I mean to teach you German, and mother and I together are going to give you splendid music lessons. We both know how you love music, and so we are sure that will be a very great pleasure to you. My only fear is that we shall never find time for half we want to do."

"Oh! dear yes;" says Philip wearily. "The days are very, very long and I never know what to do with myself when Mr. Blunt has gone, for I learn the little lessons he sets me very quickly; but I cannot manage my music alone. That vexes him, he cannot understand why I should be so stupid, he says." Then the patient boy bows his head in sore dejection, and the profound sigh he breathes comes from a very heavy heart.

As yet he has not realized the possibility of any one taking a lasting and active interest in him, his sorrows and his needs. That Lina intends to be so devoted a slave to him, as to render time short, and weariness a thing unknown, is a benefit beyond his powers of conception, and his smile still has a tinge of sadness in it, which lapses into absolute melancholy when he is left alone to ponder on his helplessness. But when Lina appeals to, rouses and encourages him as now, he turns so bright and happy a face upon her, that she feels no sacrifice on her part can be too great if it secures such cheerful satisfaction on his. The unselfish little maiden has no notion of calling her simple, pleasant duty by so grand a name as a sacrifice ; but such it decidedly is. And her total self-abnegation and sweet subjection to her helpless cousin is a bright example that many of us might be proud to follow in the service of our friends.

The first sketching expedition proved so pleasant to all concerned that it was followed by many others. The cousins set forth hand in hand, gaily following genial, even-tempered Hubert to the spot selected by him as suitable for artistic purposes. Lina did all and more than all she had originally promised. She told Philip accurately how the painting progressed, and she read him the stories of the great Magician and many others— indeed she seemed fairly on the road to the bright climax of her ambition ; for even now she often made Philip forget

that he was blind, and she certainly had
a way of shortening the hours so effectually that he began to wish there were
more of them in each quickly passing day.

Hubert Northcroft and his wife watched Lina's devotion to her cousin with
intense sympathy and profound interest.
It was a subject of constant rejoicing
to them that this bright little maid
should prove herself as steadfast and
thorough as she was fascinating. Her
sweet unselfishness more than fulfilled
their ardent wishes as to her moral
strength, and there were moments when
their pleasant impression seemed to cast
rays of light upon the undefined disc of
the distant future. As years went by it
seemed more than probable that Lina
would become daily of greater use and
service to her cousin, and thus, in due

course, each would find a willing and able helpmate at hand. What more natural or more satisfactory for all concerned than such a sequence of events?

A couple of months had been spent at Pineridge before either husband or wife dared to speak openly of the thoughts thus preoccupying them. Meanwhile the children had become constant and inseparable companions, and it would have been strange indeed if the strongest affection had not grown up in Philip's warm heart for all his newly-found relatives. Their unfailing solicitude for his welfare and the ceaseless trouble they took on his account evoked the utmost gratitude from him. His uncle, absorbed as he was in his painting, was never "too busy" to reply to the boy's eager questions, and though never talkative, seemed always inclined to afford

L 2

Philip some information which would interest or amuse the attentively listening boy. His aunt had a special claim on his affection and gratitude, because she personally superintended the music lessons which Lina now gave him every day. Music held the blind lad enthralled. His aunt's playing and Lina's singing were the chief delights of his life, and the promise that he also should play with perfect ease some day led him to practise very patiently whenever he had the chance of doing so. It was very, very hard work, painfully wearisome and discouraging at times, both for pupil and teacher; but both Aunt Letty and Lina were too well aware of the pleasure which would reward the lad's perseverance to suffer him to yield in face of the first difficulties. The matutinal hour spent at the piano, by her cousin's side,

every day, was probably the greatest test
of Lina's affection and patience; but she
bore herself bravely, and by degrees the
hardship of tuition was lessened. Everything had to be fumbled out by finger
and ear; but the fingers were acutely
sensitive, and so was the sense of hearing.
And it was so pleasant to watch his evident improvement in the art which roused
him more thoroughly than anything else
he tried to do.

But best of all was it to see the smile
of perfect content which gladdened his
gentle face if, after ceaseless repetition, he
at last managed to render a difficult phrase
accurately. That was Lina's reward; she
cared for little else now, so long as Philip
was happy.

Thus days went by, making weeks, and
weeks months, and three of these had

brought and taken the bright summer
with them, and still the Hubert Northcrofts were staying on at Pineridge, and
any suggestion of their departure was
instantly and peremptorily silenced by
Sir Stephen, who was more than reconciled
to their presence now, and regarded
it with calm but lasting satisfaction.
The concessions which under his wife's
firm guidance Hubert made to the
formalities of the house had overcome all
Sir Stephen's objections, and he had taken
an early opportunity of presenting him to
the neighbouring families, who at the close
of the London season returned to their
country houses. Hubert could not forbear
to comment on the absurd fashion which
kept the grandees prisoners in town during
the sweetest and brightest months of the
year, and sent them flocking back to the

country just as the glory of summer was on the wane and autumn tints began to show upon the falling leaves.

To Sir Stephen routine was the Alpha and Omega of social existence, and the idea of Hubert questioning the decrees of fashion appeared unseemly, not to say irreverent. But, then, Hubert always was so painfully unconventional.

The artist worked away, absorbed in his progress, and heeding outsiders or their comments not at all. He had used his time and the fine weather to the best possible advantage. He was already well forward with a large picture, and had successfully completed two smaller ones. Anxious to finish all the work begun on the spot, the painter willingly acquiesced in his brother's repeated invitations for his prolonged stay at the Priory, and made himself thoroughly

at home there. The only grievance Sir
Stephen now had against Hubert was anent
that absurd apparatus, that gipsy-like tent
which the painter had erected on a convenient mound close to the entrance of the
home park. It would be positively em-
barrassing when the county people began
to call on their return to have them gazing
at Hubert as he sat at his work out of
doors.

There really seemed to be very little
difference, the baronet thought, in the
labour of an artist and of ordinary painters
who came to renovate houses, and brought
ladders and scaffolding with them. Still
for the sake of charming Mrs. Hubert and
her pretty child, Sir Stephen resolved to
put up with his brother's vagaries, and
devoutly hoped that his friends would do
the same.

Little Lina, whose sunny influence was felt by all who came in contact with her, was gaining a remarkable ascendency over her seemingly forbidding uncle. He seldom met her on the stairs or in the passages without a smile or a word of recognition, he kissed her paternally night and morning, and when he drove to Torchester he mostly brought some souvenir home to the bonnie maid.

Far beyond all this overt recognition of her amiable spirit was the profound influence of the child on her austere relative, for he was at last, though but slowly, awakening to his son's needs.

One day he remarked to little Lina, "It is very kind and most civil of you to give yourself so much trouble about Philip, and to take pains with him as you do, but I really must protest against your inconveniencing yourself. Mr. Blunt is a very able instructor; I informed myself accurately upon that head before engaging him, and I am fully persuaded he does all that can be done."

He always addressed the child with that pompous, magisterial air of his, but that was a sign of his courtesy, and by no means implied reprimand.

"Dear uncle," she answered promptly, "I quite believe Mr. Blunt is a good teacher, but he is only a stranger, and he does not love Philip. I do; so it is no trouble to me to try and help him—indeed, it is the greatest pleasure I have."

This ingenuous rejoinder fell like a ray of light on to the baronet's dull intelligence, and he began to observe Philip and that charming guide and companion of his with quite a new interest. One day he actually commented on his son's manifest improvement by this surprising speech—

" I declare you are making quite a bright boy of him, Lina. He is as different from the dull lad you found him when first you came as day is from night."

On another occasion he repeated his satisfaction at the change effected by Lina's presence, and added—

" I could not possibly agree to your parents taking you away from us yet. The old house would be but a sorry abode if our bright fairy departed from it."

Mrs. Hubert heard this auspicious speech, and rejoiced exceedingly over its import, which she at once confided to her husband, and when the baronet, referring to it himself, suggested a compromise, by asking them all to stay over Christmas, and begin the new year at the Priory, Hubert, bearing his work in mind, assented cheerfully to his brother's gracious proposition. By the end of January the great picture would certainly be completed, and if the artist himself could not take it over to Munich, as he desired to do, it was quite possible to send it.

Mrs. Northcroft, who always gave the decisive vote on questions regarding the well-being of her family, was inclined to accept her brother-in-law's invitation, which had been repeated with unusual warmth this time. She herself had no particular desire to return to the old quasi-Bohemian existence in Munich. She was a practical woman, and a comfortable existence in a well-appointed home was thoroughly to her taste. She had perfect faith in her husband's genius, had clear-seeing Letitia, and the conviction that his work could not fail to fetch very high prices in England (when once he was duly recognised there), may have influenced her decision. From a business point of view, wealthy England was certainly preferable to impecunious Germany.

And then there was Lina's future to be considered. A return to Munich would certainly not further the plans steadily growing in Mrs. Northcroft's mind, plans which assumed strength and importance with each passing month. Hubert himself was cheerful and contented anywhere, so long as he could work in peace and was not bothered about practical affairs. He abhorred " business " and responsibility of all kinds, and invariably handed over any mental burdens thrust upon him to his willing wife. She was brave and strong, and assumed them with perfect goodwill.

"How would it be to send this picture to the Royal Academy, and give up the idea of sending it to Germany, Hugh?"

This was Letitia's pregnant suggestion one morning, after a long and critical study of her husband's most ambitious painting.

It certainly was an admirable picture. The effect of the sunset on the sturdy pine trees which formed the foreground of the landscape was marvellous. The naturally brilliant hue of the straight stems was intensified by the mellow light of the sinking orb, in which they literally glowed again, while the purple hills in the distance were sharply silhouetted against a golden sky.

Hubert was very comfortably established in a large disused room in the old wing of the Priory, which his wife had converted into a convenient studio. The small-paned window duly facing north was enlarged to a *light* of artistic dimensions, a good heat-giving stove was procured from Torchester, and fitted into the old-fashioned fireplace, rugs were spread here and there upon the stained floor, and all the appliances required by the painter were provided for him by that clever, thoughtful helpmate of his. Settled in this comfortable studio, Hubert felt very much at his ease, and he worked with surprising diligence through-out the short winter days, appreciating and doing full justice to the precious day-light hours.

That well-considered proposition of his wife's anent his last and greatest effort roused the artist's dormant ambition. To have painted a Torshire landscape in Eng-land and to send it straight to London for exhibition was indeed a happy and inspiring thought; and with that end in view Hubert's remarkable zeal and freshly-aroused energy grew in proportion to the lessening number of days left him for completing his masterpiece.

Thus all went brightly and prosperously at the Priory, until a sudden gloom was cast over the inhabitants by the severe indisposition of cheerful Mrs. Hubert. The winter was most inclement, and in her frequent visits of charity to some of the old and sick in the village, the kind-hearted lady had caught a severe cold, which led to rheumatic fever, and prostrated her completely. She kept her bed throughout the month of January, and when she at last reappeared at luncheon Sir Stephen expressed himself profoundly shocked by the change in her appearance ; indeed he displayed the greatest concern about her, and solemnly adjured Hubert to get better advice. The easy-going artist was suddenly amazed and alarmed. No anxiety had hitherto penetrated his great love for his wife. He had a vague impression that nothing could ever ail her or seriously interfere with the manifold services she rendered him. But when his brother drew his attention to the fact that Mrs. Hubert was undoubtedly very ill still, and that the doctor from Torchester could not have understood her case, then Hubert instantly desired to consult the first physician in England. Was not Sir Joseph Barry a great authority, might he not be telegraphed for at once ?

The great physician speedily answered Hubert's urgent summons. He arrived at Torchester by the express train that afternoon.

"There is no immediate danger," he said, compressing his thin lips and knitting his brows mysteriously, "and there was certainly not the slightest necessity for a telegram, a letter would have been as effective, and spared me a considerable amount of inconvenience."

The master of Pineridge apologized with the greatest courtesy for his brother's "inconsiderate precipitancy," and blamed himself for leaving Hubert to do anything on his own account. He was bound to blunder whenever he attempted to follow his rash impulses.

"There are no grave symptoms at present," repeated the oracle, when he had paid a second visit to the patient, who had retired to her room again, and

was seated in an arm chair by the fire
there. Sir Joseph Barry had been
mentally and physically refreshed by a
few hours' rest and an excellent dinner,
and he evidently took a more cheerful
view of things in general. "At the same
time," he continued, fixing Hubert with
that solemn penetrating gaze for which
he was famous, "at the same time I
am bound to tell you that your wife
requires the greatest care and attention.
It appears to me"—and here the grave
physician became doubly impressive,
—"it appears to me that the lady has
some mental preoccupation, some occult
anxiety which weighs on her spirits and
deprives her of the tranquillity so essential to her perfect recovery. Are you
aware of any reason whatever for the
mental distress I apprehend?"

Hubert declared himself quite ignorant of any such disturbing influence in his dear wife's case, and the doctor, perceiving her loving husband's evident trouble, changed his portentous tone, and briefly repeated certain directions as to the patient's present treatment. "I will see her again in a week or two," he said. "I wish it were possible for you to bring her up to London for a time. I could form a more decided opinion if I saw her frequently. Meanwhile keep her from fretting. She must have no anxiety, no brooding. That is a *sine quâ non* for her ultimate recovery. After so severe an attack of rheumatic fever, we may always fear for the heart. A cheerful mental condition is the safest and surest antidote. Care kills more folks than statisticians have ever heard of."

Poor Hubert! it was not destined that he, more than the rest of mortals, should lead an untroubled existence. He complained bitterly of the " terrible things " that were always happening to somebody. There was poor old Stephen, who had a blind son ; now there was dear " useful Letty " a helpless invalid. Why should people have so much bother in this troublesome world ? Why could not he at least be left to paint in peace ? But what was the use of fretting and worry ?

Meanwhile he contrived to get rid of his particular share in the world's troubles by issuing tremendous sighs and volumes of tobacco smoke ; and what was far more effectual in dispersing the clouds of perplexity which so suddenly overwhelmed him, he worked on with unremitting assiduity, and actually succeeded in completing his great picture within the time he had allowed himself. A move should be made to London, and—at once, if it were only for the sake of proximity to the skilled physician who had undertaken to watch Mrs. Hubert's perplexing case.

CHAPTER IX

THE picture was sent to the Royal Academy, and, strange as it may seem for those days (being "only a landscape"), it was well hung. More than that, it brought a crowd of fresh commissions to the painter. Letitia's foresight was gratefully acknowledged by improvident Hubert, and the thought of returning to the Continent finally abandoned. A house, with a good studio as *annexe,* was secured on the breezy, and then thoroughly rural, heights of Hampstead, and as this house had been built and furnished by a painter, who was taking his work and his family abroad for

some years, the Northcrofts found their
new home thoroughly suitable in every
respect. The change was evidently beneficial to Mrs. Hubert, whose health soon
showed signs of improvement, and
though a strange languor and a striking
pallor remained to tell of the shock
her system had received in the course
of that prolonged, wearing illness, she
was gradually returning to her former
condition, and soon managed to fulfil
her onerous duties with the old zealous
spirit, if not with her wonted activity.
"Peace of mind, cheerful society, no
fretting, no brooding," repeated Sir
Joseph Barry, again and again, and he
always looked at Hubert with that
grave, penetrating gaze which was more
eloquent even than his impressive words.
He was constantly assured that there was

nothing, nothing indeed, to disturb his patient's security; but there was an air of incredulity in the shake of his venerable head, and his reply was the frequent repetition of his first warning to Hubert—"Keep her mind at ease, and above all else remember that any sudden excitement, or any severe mental shock, might bring about the most disastrous consequences."

Hubert heard; but his was not an anxious disposition, and he thought he could see no cause for alarm, while his dear Letty herself endeavoured to assure him that she was getting on splendidly, that she had never been better, and that doctors always liked to make a fuss, of course, or else their skill in curing people would not be sufficiently appreciated.

The parting between the cousins was

a terrible grief to them both, and the sorrow consequent upon it was lasting. All the elders did their utmost to comfort the children, and repeated promises were made as to Philip's coming to stay at the new house in London, and Lina's speedy return to the Priory on another long visit with her parents. But the blank she left in the lad's life completely prostrated him for a time. The sad helplessness of his condition was a thousand times more painful to him now than it had ever been before. As a child he had borne his affliction with a patient and not uncheerful docility; but Lina's tender care and patient devotion had aroused all the responsive faculties of his nature, and these loving instincts refused to be quelled now. He positively rebelled against the terrible pain Lina's

absence gave him, he cried out about
his suffering as though it were causing
him absolute physical pain. What was
to become of the studies on which they
had so earnestly entered together? Were
all the numerous pursuits and occupations
to come to a sudden end? Those happy
pastimes, in which Lina had lent him her
eyes, her hands, and the most watchful
attention, until he often forgot that he
was not as others were; was he to give
up all that made life worth living, all
that compensated him for the beauties of
nature, the delights of study, and the
relaxation so necessary to the young?
Oh! it was sad, sad, terrible, not to be
endured. The only resource left him
was his music, and even there Lina's
sudden absence checkmated his efforts.
How could he go on working, improving,

since he was deprived of her watchful surveillance? So morbid, so profoundly melancholy, was the lad, that it was well the thought of suicide never presented itself to him. In his condition of mental desolation death would have seemed preferable to life without Lina.

What comfort he did find, poor fellow, was in the diligent perusal of his precious Bible, the comforting truths of which had become better appreciated by him since Mrs. Northcroft had had many a loving, serious, but hopeful talk with him on matters she deemed of the highest importance herself, and which she firmly believed necessary to the peace of mind of every human being. She was indeed a truly religious woman, and her life was an embodiment of that sweet charity which she so urgently and persistently strove to inculcate in every one about her, and which she herself practised faithfully, often under the most adverse circumstances.

Sir Stephen, a little more alive than of yore to his son's sad condition and innumerable needs, condescended to argue with him on the subject of his exaggerated grief. He had caught a glimpse of the poor lad one day, as he sat in the old attitude of helpless dejection, his head bowed low upon his breast, his hands hanging listlessly at his side. This pitiable sight inspired the father with a sense of compunction; for it brought to his mind the time when Philip was always dull, and also reminded him of the extent of the change Lina had wrought in that sadly isolated life.

"You know, Philip, that it is perfectly preposterous your giving yourself all these airs of desolation," says Sir Stephen, suddenly entering his son's room, after he had stood on the threshold awhile, making mental notes on his dejected appearance. As he looked, a sense akin to pity animated him; but when he addresses the boy his manner is as forbidding, his tone as hard as ever—"You surely are old enough by this time to comprehend the fitness of things to some extent? How can you possibly expect that Lina is always to be at your beck and call?"

Philip makes a deprecating movement with his long expressive hands, and his head sinks lower and lower upon his breast; but he gives no audible rejoinder to his father's tirade.

There is a pause—pensive on one side, threatening on the other, and after a while the latter ends in these sharply spoken words—

" You are both unreasonable and absurd in supposing that you can treat your cousin like a hired servant, a professional reader paid so much an hour for services rendered. Why, even Mr. Blunt would rebel at the multifarious duties you expected Lina to fulful at your bidding."

An extraordinary change comes over Philip's face while his father is speaking. He turns gradually but awfully pale, and as he rises and moves a step toward his parent he is visibly trembling.

" A servant, father? How can you suggest that I expected menial services from my kindest, dearest and best friend? Can you for one moment suppose that any paid person would do for me what Lina did? I am shocked, and hurt too, at the view you take of her—and of me."

"Do not excite yourself, do not talk nonsense, boy, and, before all else, have the goodness to remember to whom you are addressing yourself. Is that the tone befitting a son who appeals to his father?"

Sir Stephen is fairly taken aback. He can hardly trust his own power of hearing. He had never struck the latent steel in his boy's soul, and had deemed him utterly incapable of any sort of fire. But that quivering lip, the trembling hands, and the defiant attitude plainly show how effectually Philip is roused at last; and when his father realizes the full extent of the conflagration he has brought about, he feels somewhat alarmed.

"Sit down, my boy," he says, in a

pacifying tone. "I perceive that you are not aware yourself of the impropriety of speech into which excitement has betrayed you. Let us speak quietly, comfortably together, and devise some method by which you can be interested and amused in future. Your recent loneliness has evidently preyed upon your spirits. You are quite morbid to-day."

Sir Stephen pauses for the encouragement of a reply; but he is disappointed. Philip sits silent and motionless. He offers neither apology for his past rudeness nor further protest. He listens passively to the next proposition made to him—

"I have resolved in any case to put some person entirely at your disposal as reader, guide, and secretary," says Sir Stephen; "and, as you evidently incline to female companionship, you shall be humoured in that respect also. Mrs. Ruskett tells me that she has struggled hard to give her daughter a good education, and the girl is about to return home after two years' residence in a high-class boarding-school. An exemplary parent a worthy woman that Mrs. Ruskett—under the circumstances—no better or more useful servant could possibly be found for you than this Isabel. I will consult the housekeeper on the spot. I am sure my proposal will meet with her approbation. She is devoted to our family, and it will gratify her to think that, while she is serving the head of the house, her daughter is able to attend upon the heir-apparent."

Sir Stephen actually attempts to be jocular. He enunciates the last words with a humorous intonation, but Philip is in no mood to smile at jokes or to appreciate unwelcome favours. There is a resentful curve about his lips, as he relapses into his former attitude of passive endurance. He by no means approves of his father's suggestions; but he is too weary, too sick at heart, for further protest of any kind.

Mrs. Ruskett, who had laboured under incessant anxiety that those "'Uberts" would interfere in her plans, was immensely relieved at their unexpected and most welcome departure.

"Good riddance of bad rubbish, indeed!" she remarked to Mr. Grind, and they both enjoyed a glass of fine old port as they drank to the "long stay away of those meddlesome relations of the master's."

"I shall have my child back from

school now," said Mrs. Sarah, smacking her lips, " and we'll soon see if a high-spirited English lady, who has had the best of education at a first-class boarding school, can't hold her own with Master Philip quite as well, or a deal better, most likely, than that yellow-haired Miss Lina, who made up to her poor cousin in the most bold-faced manner, and took every advantage of his being blind, and consequently at her mercy ! "

In pursuance of the deeply-laid plan of her own, Mrs. Ruskett awaited a favourable opportunity to make certain suggestions to her austere master, and one day when she found him alone in the library, she had ventured to inform him of the intended return of her daughter from school, and added some information as to the excellent education she had managed to give that young lady.

"I am most anxious to find her some suitable occupation," the wily housekeeper added, pleadingly. "Her schooling has cost me far more money than a poor woman like me is well able to afford; but now the dear girl must try to pay me back by earning a little something on her own account." And then she warily proceeded to suggest that Master Philip would be lonesome-like now Miss Lina had gone, and that such help and companionship as he required, her daughter would be quite able and most delighted to offer him.

"My poor child tried hard to be of service to the young gentleman when both of them were children," she urged, "and of course she could do 'undreds of things now that she had never dreamt of before her education was complete."

At this extensive assertion Sir Stephen smiled just a little, and Mrs. Sarah began to feel very hopeful about the success of her scheme.

"There's only one thing I am afraid of in making this proposal to my kind master, Sir Stephen," the woman added pleadingly, as she was about to leave the room.

"And that is?" he asked, pleased by her extreme deference.

"Things may be changed now both is older," she said; "but years ago Master Philip did not take to my poor child at all, and that went nigh to break her heart, the darling, for she is of a loving and amiable turn is my Isabel." A suppressed sob pointed this speech, and of all these words and signs Sir Stephen took special heed.

A few dull, monotonous days followed that amazing demonstration of passion on Philip's part before his father ventured to allude to the subject of their discussion again, and then he quietly announced that he had definitively settled and arranged all matters with Mrs. Ruskett now, and that the girl Isabel would arrive at Pineridge, and be prepared to commence her duties as reader and amanuensis on the Monday following.

But, instead of being grateful to his father for this most considerate propo-sition, the lad received it with evident disgust; indeed, he resented the notion of Isabella Ruskett's service with an indig-nant protest, and solemnly declared that he could *never*, *never*, *never!* derive the smallest comfort or consolation from so unpromising a scheme. He was, however, powerless to prevent his elders from carrying out what they chose to consider essential to his comfort, and the very morning after Isabel's arrival at the Priory her mother settled her in "Master Philip's study," and bade her read aloud to the "poor dear young gentleman."

This brought Philip's rising rebellion to a climax. He burst into a torrent of wild words and passionate irritation. He fled from the study, and trembling in every limb, presented himself, white in face, wild in manner, before his astonished father.

"That girl's reading is too dreadful, it hurts me, it hurts me, I cannot bear it," cried the unhappy boy, and then he tried to explain to his indignant parent the suffering caused to him by Isabel's affectation, her strident tones, her mincing articulation, her utter disregard of all punctuation, and her wilful emphasis on every substantive. The contrast between this creature's tone of voice, her obstructive presence, and her affected manner, and Lina's gentle, sympathetic companionship, was too terrible ; and Philip, smarting painfully under the infliction, declared he could bear no more of it.

"I would ten thousand times rather be quite alone and never hear another word read to me at all," cried the boy, standing before his father and wringing his hands in despair as he made his protestation. "I cannot listen to that dreadful girl again ! "

Philip's former passion had warned Sir Stephen that a second outbreak might be expected, and yet he was taken by surprise again at the lad's angry vehemance. He called him undutiful, ungrateful, disobedient, unfilial, and heaped up one opprobrious epithet on another, but without any appreciable result. It was not until more than a month of alternate reproof, threat, and persuasion had made the blind boy feel himself a martyr, and cruelly persecuted, that he was at last reduced to a state of something like quiescence.

Mrs. Ruskett acted the part of presiding genius, and seized upon the first favourable moment in which there seemed a chance of again inducting her daughter as companion to the heir apparent.

Wearied by prolonged resistance, gentle Philip suffered the girl's occasional presence in silence, if not in patience; but that he did suffer was very evident, and his moral depression soon acted detrimentally upon his health. The old languor overcame him with tenfold vigour. He even hated the hours with Mr. Blunt now, which once were welcomed so eagerly as breaks in the long monotonous days; and, worse still, his music lessons ceased to have any charm in them, since they brought Lina's absence more vividly and painfully to his mind than aught else.

Mr. Blunt, though uncultured, was not without feeling, and after watching his pupil with considerable anxiety for a couple of months, he became seriously alarmed about his morbid condition.

At last the tutor actually summoned up courage enough to hint at the nature and extent of his uneasiness to the autocratic master of Pineridge. This was a *maurais quart-d'heure* for both men, but it had an excellent result for the innocent cause of their discussion, who was soon told that Mr. Blunt, before very long, was to take him to London to spend a few weeks at his uncle Hubert's new house.

That news wrought a sudden but wonderful change in the lad. Languor and indifference vanished as heavy clouds do before the rising sun. The mist of sorrow was dispersed, and joy—the joy of bright anticipation—asserted its hopeful sway. Even Isabel was endured in the study now, for the ice of displeased reserve was broken, and Philip was in a measure thankful to have some one near him to whom he might talk of the prospect before him. He was actually willing to take Isabel's arm now, and to go for walks with her through the garden and shrubberies. And sometimes they went up along the high road, and the lanes which led to the great pine wood on the borders of Tor and Westshire, for as they were walking they could talk, and a month's visit to London paid to a friend by Isabel just after she left school formed a theme of incessant discussion between them. Miss Ruskett had spent the time of her stay in the metropolis with a cousin who was a dresser at one of the principal theatres, and from this person (Jane Hopkins by name) the girl had obtained much theatrical information as to life behind the scenes, together with many passes for the pit on various occasions. To Philip, whose active mind had been freshly aroused by the promise of going to town so soon, Isabel's lively accounts of the wonders of the metropolis presented

a new and engrossing subject of interest.
He now asked far more questions than
even Miss Ruskett felt inclined to answer.
And yet she was flattered by the intense
satisfaction with which Sir Stephen's son
listened to her whom, a few week's ago, he
had treated with such scant consideration.
She felt sorry the young gentleman was
blind, because he could not see her. It
seemed a shame that her "wicked black
eyes," which had brought her no end of
compliments already, should be invisible
to him, and so deeply did she commiserate
his inability to admire her new silk dress
(the one with a train to it) that she gave
him the most elaborate description of its
fit, texture, and appearance.

He was wondering while she spoke
whether Lina's dresses were likely to be
made in a similar fashion, and earnestly

strove to picture the general effect of such costume and colours with his mental vision, and then he asked his companion for further details as to her personal appearance. Now Isabel was quite in her element, and the portrait she painted of herself in glowing words would have done honour to Terbourg himself, so elaborate were its details, so loving the lingering touches on the glossy, black hair, the brilliant complexion, and "wicked eyes."

Philip listened in wondering patience. An earnest desire to improve his knowledge of the appearance of things around him kept him silent and attentive, and he was striving to make mental comparisons, while Miss Ruskett discoursed of her beauty with wondrous volubility.

"You are dark, then?" asked Philip,

having arrived at some conclusion at last, "and my cousin is what they call fair?"

"Yes," answers Isabel viciously. My ma told me Miss Lina was one of your quiet deep sort, and they have never much to boast of in looks or colour either. Your cousin, from all I have heard, must be just as different from me as day is from night."

"I am sure of it," says Philip with startling emphasis, and mentally continues, "Thank God that is so!"

Miss Ruskett resents the tone of his assertion, and takes the trouble to explain to him that a brilliant night with "lots" of lamps, gay dresses, and plenty of music, such as she beheld at a *fête* on the London stage, is far more attractive to those who can see than any daylight scene could ever be. "And that is just the difference there is between a dashing sort of girl like me and one of the fair, goody-goody sort such as your cousin seems to have made you think she is."

"I quite understand you," says Philip quietly. In his heart he adds, "and the more I know you, the less I like you; but I loved Lina better and better day after day, and since I am to be so soon with her again, and quite happy, I can listen even to you in patience now."

CHAPTER X

ON THE HEIGHTS OF HAMPSTEAD.

IN 1859 Hampstead Heath was still an eminently rural tract of country, and when Hubert took possession of the comfortable, old-fashioned red-brick house vacated by the brother artist of whom he was to rent it, he found himself thoroughly at his ease there. The studio, which had but lately been built as an annexe, had every modern convenience, and the views from the upper windows and from the heath beyond the garden were full of suggestions to the painter's mind. Mrs. Hubert was decidedly better and stronger for the change; her husband thoroughly content, and not a little pleased to be his own master once more and free from the supervision of his ceremonious brother. Lina was the only one of the trio who did not delight in their change of abode. She missed her blind cousin every hour in the day; even the visits of her daily governess, and the lessons of Herr Lirtz, her singing-master, failed to supply the vacuum in her life which her constant care for Philip had so abundantly filled. Sometimes she wrote him a letter, but that after all was scant consolation to either, for the letter would have to be read aloud by some unsympathetic third person, who neither felt with, nor for, the enthusiastic correspondent. How could she pour out the inmost thoughts of her young loving heart, the thousand questions, hints, and suggestions dictated by her intimate knowledge of his wants, wishes, and likings, while the chilling conviction that alien eyes would read her words before they reached his ears, checked her at every sentence?

Oh! if she could but print all she longed to tell him in the regulation embossed letters,—and, if then she could be sure that he, and he alone, would unravel the loving words she so ardently longed to say to her afflicted darling!

She pined visibly, poor little maid. This enforced absence from one who had absorbed her every thought, and required her constant and ceaseless attention, changed the happy current of her unselfish life, and she ceased to find pleasure or contentment in anything. Indeed she was but a degree less impatient than poor Philip himself at their protracted separation. For though Sir Stephen had pacified his son by the promise of a speedy visit to London, week after week, and month after month, actually went by before there were any signs of the realization of the meeting to which the cousins so anxiously looked forward. The summer waned, autumn tints appeared upon the trees and shrubs on the heath at Hampstead, and in the gardens of Pineridge. Philip, though bitterly disappointed at the protracted delay of his journey, still firmly believed in its ultimate possibility, and, as we have seen, when it was once definitely settled on, through the friendly intercession of Mr. Blunt and Sir Stephen, consoled himself, after a fashion, by dwelling on the delights which it would yield and by accepting with what grace he could the assistance and companionship of Isabel Ruskett.

Hubert Northcroft and his wife were by no means unobservant of the change in their precious Lina, and began to speak to one another more openly than they had hitherto done, of the future result of the profound and lasting, though as yet childish and unacknowledged love of the young cousins.

Sir Stephen occasionally wrote a letter to his brother, and of course he alluded to the blank caused in his son's life by Lina's absence, and the perplexities which this had produced in his (the baronet's) mind. But he still made very light of the blind boy's grievances, and dwelt at some length on the admirable plan that had been adopted for his assistance. " Mrs. Ruskett's daughter now fills the onerous post of reader and servant to my son, to the perfect satisfaction of all concerned." This was Sir Stephen's off-hand fashion of disposing of Philip's troubles and difficulties, but clear-sighted Letitia was not deceived by his tone, and felt as ever the keenest pity for her lonely, afflicted nephew. Philip, himself, from time to time dictated letters to his aunt or his cousin; but these were mostly written by the matter-of-fact Mr. Blunt. Once, and once only, was Miss Isabel's pen pressed into this service, for Philip shrank intuitively from doing anything which appeared to associate that young person with his sweet Lina. The letter was addressed to Miss Northcroft, but so far from giving her pleasure, it filled her with sorrow and misgiving. Instead of treasuring it in the little sandalwood work-box in which the rest of Philip's variously written epistles were

safely locked up, she tore this last letter
into shreds, flung them out of the open
window of her little chamber at the top
of the house, and watched the pieces
whirling and eddying like autumn leaves
on the back of the north wind, **away**
away, and away—out of sight.   Out of
mind she hoped.   From the day she
received that letter, Lina hated mauve
ink ; and the pointed writing suggestive
of pins, which, in those days, was
deemed " elegant " in young ladies'
schools, became her lasting aversion.
The difficulty which hampered poor Lina
in her desire to correspond with her
cousin, appeared to him more than
trebled in his own case.   How could he
dictate to any outsider the tender little
confidences meant for her loving ear
alone ?   How could he confide to any

third person his intense longing for the renewal of their happy and satisfactory companionship? She understood him thoroughly. That he knew well, and it gave him strength and comfort. But others? . . . .

All others would sneer if he bade them write exactly what he wished to tell her. His father would probably bid him write sense, if he wrote at all, and ask him not to deliver himself of the farrago of sentimental nonsense with which his brain teemed whenever he thought of his Lina. Mr. Blunt would suggest a concise and matter-of-fact form of expression, and would certainly construe "My own darling Lina," into "Dear Cousin!" No, Philip could not, and would not, be satisfied with this vicarious mode of expressing his inmost sacred feelings. And so it came to pass that his letters grew few and far between, until he suddenly wrote (per Mr. Blunt) that it was now positively arranged that that gentleman, who was going to spend his Christmas holidays in London, should bring his pupil up to Hampstead *en route.*

"So I shall, after all, be with you before this miserable year comes to its sad end," was the concluding sentence of the boy's dictated letter. "And on the picturesque heights above London, of which dear Aunt Letty has given me so vivid a picture, I shall hope to get over the weary loneliness of the wretched months I have spent since all you bright people deserted Pineridge.

"Your loving

"Philip."

When the day and hour of her cousin's arrival had been finally settled, Lina's unnatural apathy was changed into eager excitement, as by the wave of a magician's wand. Her previous indifference gave place to tumultuous delight, and she could scarcely restrain her exuberant spirits within the bounds of decorum even during the solemn lesson hours which she gleefully anticipated Philip would, ere long, share with her again. She proposed walking to the station to meet him. And failing to obtain her mother's consent to this adventurous exploit, she implored permission to run down steep Haverstock Hill to meet the cab on its upward climb.

"But you must miss it in the dusk, my darling, and that would never do," suggested Hubert, smiling in placid wonder at the child's excitement. So, poor Lina had perforce to content herself with the ancient panacea that affords such scanty consolation to any young soul —patience! patience! Nevertheless, at intervals she danced to and fro with wild ectasy on the gravel walk within the old iron gates, and now and then she escaped and ran a yard or two along the high road beyond.

At last!

Yes, at last wheels are heard slowly advancing, and the cumbersome luggage-laden cab stops, with Mr. Blunt and Philip inside, while the driver commences a hoarse inquiry in which the name "Northcroft" alone is intelligible.

"Yes, it is all right. Stop! It is here! here!" cries Lina, jubilant. And in another instant, regardless of father, mother, tutor, or driver, the child has seized the handle of the cab door, which she opens with the utmost alacrity.

"I'll help you, I'll hold you—only one step. Take care, Philip, my dear, my dearest, my darling cousin!"

The boy and girl are locked close in one another's arms. Tears are running over their cheeks, joy is beating wildly in their happy young hearts—the long, bitter ordeal of separation is over, they are united once more, and wholly content.

* * * * *

The happiness of the simple household at Hampstead was completed by the advent of "dear cousin Philip." The original proposition was that he should spend Christmas with his beloved relatives; but he stayed on and on. First, "to see the New Year in," then to await more settled weather, after the breaking of an unusually prolonged frost, and finally because he was a welcome and delighted guest, for whose protracted stay no reason was needed beyond the indispensable facts, that he was happy to be with his good friends, and that they rejoiced to see him in their midst.

The success which had attended Hubert as an exhibitor the previous year, in the Royal Academy, was sufficient encouragement for his sending still more important work this following season of 1860.

The excitement, the hurly-burly, which attends the commencement of the London Art-year, was much the same twenty years ago as it is in these days; for history repeats itself, and the opening of the Royal Academy, in Trafalgar Square then, was a very similar occasion to the opening of the great picture show in Piccadilly now.

In his way, blind Philip loves pictures, and of course he must pay a visit to the Exhibition. Hubert and Lina have so far trained him that he follows their detailed descriptions with keenest interest, and in the studio he *feels* his way to a knowledge of the subject on the easel, by having his forefinger carefully guided over the out line of composition and by pausing to reflect as each succeeding point is minutely described to him. Hence, an expedition to the Royal Academy, during the mouth of May, becomes one of the most marked episodes in the life at Hampstead, and although Hubert and his wife have been to the private view, the former consents, somewhat reluctantly, to go again, and act as escort to his daughter and nephew. Reluctantly, be it said, because the artist has the greatest objection to the heat, dust, and hubbub of the crowded rooms, and grudges even an hour of the bright summer weather spent away from his own airy abode.

The first novelty which produces a vivid impression on Philip, on the occasion of his first visit to the Academy, is the sound of the sentries relieving guard in front of the National Gallery. The soldiers' measured tread, the clank of arms, the description of their appearance, all combine to arrest his attention, and Lina has to answer questions innumerable before Philip has made himself thoroughly acquainted with this unexpected phenomenon. When he is sufficiently instructed on that head, he relapses in puzzled silence, and as the trio make their way up the broad stone steps, and enter the crowded rooms, Philip listens eagerly to the stray words and comments so rapidly bandied from right to left. It is not long before Hubert begins to grumble at the terrible heat, the stifling dust, and the troublesome, pushing people. The blind lad is exceedingly anxious to ascertain the exact position of his uncle's pictures, and is evidently gratified when he finds his fingers placed upon the frames of two which hang upon the line.

"As for the third, Phil," says the artist, laughing, " the Academicians have thought *that* far too precious for the vulgar gaze, so they have considerately skyed it—hoisted it out of sight, you understand—and whoever wishes to see it must use an opera-glass or a telescope."

While Lina explains this bit of her father's facetiousness to her cousin, a friend of the former touches him unexpectedly on the arm. The stranger is an artist, and Hubert hails his advent as a blessed relief, for he has come to the end of his patience, though Lina, who is intensely interested in the novelty of the sights presented to her, shows no signs of weariness as yet.

"I particularly want your opinion on that landscape of Dove's, Northcroft," says Beech, the friend. "There is quite a whirlwind of discussion about it among the R. A.s generally, and the outsiders in particular. I, for my part, contend it is not true. You just come and look at it with me; I am sure the sky is several tones too low."

"Ah, well; I hope it's not far off,"

says Hubert wearily; "for to tell you the truth Beech, I am sick of pictures, and tired to death by the crowd, the worry, and the noise."

"It's in the farthest room, unluckily," says Beech; "but I am personally interested in it, and I have faith in your judgment, so do come, it won't take you a minute."

"Oh! of course!" sighs Hubert, with a comic air of resignation.

"Can you find me a seat here, while they go on, Lina?" whispers Philip; "my head begins to ache with the noise and heat. I will wait for you: don't say you are going to stay with me, because I should prefer your seeing all you possibly can: this may be your only chance."

Lina demurs.

"Can I leave you?" she says doubtfully."

"Set me down near the entrance," he says, "where I can get a little air. I shall be quite safe, and then you must take a good look round those rooms we have not been into, and come and report progress to me. I do want you to see as much as possible for my sake."

"Well, have you settled it between you, my dears, who comes and who stays?" asks Hubert; "we shall not take ten minutes over the business of inspection, I promise you, for I cannot stand any more of this crowd."

Lina establishes the blind lad comfortably on a bench near the head of the stairs, as he had suggested, and, with a loving pressure of his hand, she leaves him, while she follows the two artists, who saunter slowly on, absorbed in talking " shop " to their hearts' content.

* * * * *

" Good gracious me, Mr. Philip, who ever would have thought of seeing you here ! Why, at first I could hardly believe my eyes ! " says a shrill voice close to his ear; and the owner of the voice possesses herself eagerly of the hand that lies on the blind lad's knee.

Philip recognises Miss Ruskett's tones at once, but the knowledge that she has seated herself by his side affords him no kind of satisfaction.

" What has brought you to town, Isabel ? " he presently asks, after an awkward pause.

" Ah ! you may well be surprised, Mr.

Philip," she answers with that affected laugh which she has copied from a certain burlesque actress. "I came up partly on business and partly on pleasure; but I want to hear all you have been doing; tell me something about yourself, now do. Ma will be pleased to think I have met you. She did wish me to call up at Hampstead; but that's such a long journey, and I never seem to have a minute to spare as it is. I am staying with Mrs. Hopkins—cousin Jane, you know, I told you all about her—do you remember?" Philip nods assent and vaguely wonders how he ever could have listened to this uncultured girl with anything like interest or amusement. She certainly bores him exceedingly now. "Is your cousin with you to-day?" he asks, pining for relief.

"Oh, dear, yes," says Isabel, laughing aloud again; she is standing waiting for me; and now she is making signs to me to come away. Ha, ha! She's cross because she thinks I'm wasting her time while I'm up to my larks, flirting with a handsome young stranger. She knows my ways by this time; though she has no idea that you can't even see whether I'm pretty or plain." Here follows the stage laugh, and Philip is thankful that Lina had left him before this demonstrative young lady appeared upon the scene. No wonder that her voice falls discordantly upon his sensitive ear, while Lina's gentle tones are still vibrating in his memory.

"Don't fidget," says Isabel sharply, seeing him inclined to edge away from her side; "I have heaps of things to say to you. It seems a year since we had a regular good chat together. But perhaps you don't care to talk to me now, since you have been used to the company of Miss Lina; pretty care milady seems to take of you too—my word! nice considerate people you've got to look after you. Fancy their leaving you all by yourself in such a crowd as this! *shameful*, that's what I call it!"

Some latent personal grievance lends emphasis to Isabel's protest; but Philip can bear no more.

"My friends have placed me here by my own request," he says angrily. "You must not suppose—I will not allow you to question their conduct in any way. They are always kind, gentle, and considerate to me."

"Oh! I'm sure I beg your pardon very

humbly, Mr. Philip," says Isabel, with a wild attempt at satire; "I quite forgot! of course, whatever Miss Lina does *must* be right. I stand corrected; I might have remembered that she is perfect in your ideas is that mysterious young lady whom I never manage to get a glimpse of. When she was at the Priory I was away, and *vice versâ*, as they say in the classics! Still, I do wonder at *her* leaving you here by yourself. I thought she was so extra careful of you. My ma always said that when Sir Stephen was by, there was never an end to her billing and cooing. Perhaps that was for the benefit of your pa. There, there, don't look so grumpy, Mr. Philip. It's only my chaff of course. You ought to know me better than to be cross at my nonsensical chatter.

She moves closer to him, and pats his arm with her fan, as she whispers: " But now I *do* wish you'd tell me whatever you came here for? Fancy a blind young gentleman coming to see the pictures. Oh! Jane, this is a joke; just come here,—"

Isabel beckons to Mrs. Hopkins, who approaches slowly and makes a warning sign to her relative to curb her tongue and her laughter; for the passers-by linger, looking and wondering at the bold, black-eyed girl who has laid her yellow-gloved hand on the arm of that gentle, melancholy lad, who seems to appreciate her attentions so little.

"Jane here can tell you that not seeing the pictures is no loss," continues Isabel, subduing her tone somewhat, but informing her cousin in an audible aside,—

"It's Mr. Philip, Sir Stephen's son and heir, he's quite blind, don't you know?"

"Lor!" exclaims Mrs. Hopkins, and being good-natured, adds, "No, indeed, sir, the pictures are no loss I can assure you; it makes my head whirl to look at them. We came to see the people, and they ain't much to look at neither; so you needn't fret sir, I'm sure."

"Oh! I love a crowd," remarks Isabel, "and we are going to the play to-night. Have you been to the theatre yet, Mr. Philip?" He shakes his head.

"We had better be going, my dear," here interposes Mrs. Hopkins; "orders are not admitted after seven, and we must go over to the Waterloo road first, and that's a good step from here. I want my tea, too, I'm that thirsty."

"Well, I suppose I must say good-bye,

then, Mr. Philip," says Isabel, hastily;
"it won't do to be late at the Kaleidoscope. That's the style of theatre *I* like.
Such handsome dresses; such cheeky girls.
One gentleman, a friend of mine, who
belongs to the company, says I should do
well if I joined them. I have just the
right face and figure, and should be sure
to get on. I shall wait and see. Don't
you say a word to ma, please, Mr. Philip,
but I have half a mind to try my luck
on the stage."

"Come along, Isa, do," urges Mrs.
Hopkins. "I know we shall be late."

"I should have liked to wait and see
that goody-goody cousin of yours," repeats Miss Ruskett as she rises. "The
most considerate young lady who brings
you to *see* the pictures—ha! ha!—and
then leaves you all by your poor blind

self. Ta-ta, or *au revoir*, as Ma'amselle taught us to say for politeness. Give my respects—ahem—to Miss Lina, and tell her to look after you better in future, or I must go and stay at Hampstead and divide the duty with her."

*　　*　　*　　*　　*

Yes; she has really gone at last. The rustle of a stiff crinoline, the clank of high-heeled boots, the obtrusive motion of a crackling fan, are all lost in the surging crowd which carries them away. And Philip, intensely relieved, finds himself alone once more.

He dreaded Lina's return while that noisy girl was beside him, holding his hand, and laughing in his face. He begins to long for the sound of the sweet familiar voice which has made all others sound unmusical to him.

"Dear Phil," that voice whispers presently, close to his ear, "have we been very long away? Mr. Beech had so much to say, and father stood talking, talking too. I was in despair at last, and begged leave to run back and see after you. Philip, dear, are you vexed?"

Lina's quick eyes, accustomed to note every movement of his face and hands, at once detects that something has distressed him. But a strange feeling seals the boy's lips. He hates the thought of mentioning the name of Isabel to his cousin; he knows, though he cannot say why, that she would not like to hear it.

"Oh, I am only a little tired of all this noise and bustle," he answers, wearily. "Is uncle ready; may we go out into the fresh air now?"

"So you have had enough of the Academy, too, have you, Phil?" asks Hubert, cheerily. He has overheard his nephew's last words. "Sensible lad," he adds; "let us get out at once under God's pure sky, and leave the benighted rabble behind us."

CHAPTER XI

PHILIP had come to Hampstead to stay two months and actually remained more than a year. A bright, prosperous, and happy year that, which in the days to come he looked back upon as the one pleasant spot of verdure in the desert of his barren life. Twice in the course of those twelve months his uncle and Lina went home to Pineridge with him; but Mrs. North-croft preferred to remain at Hampstead, and welcomed her " truant trio " back with evident delight. She seemed to dread the brother-in-law now, who had at one time inspired her with so little awe. Perhaps this nervous apprehension was due to her more susceptible condition of mind and body; perhaps she had learnt in the course of years to understand the exceeding hardness of his character, and the deep-seated prejudice of his convictions, more thoroughly than on the pleasant occasion of her first visit. Lina and her stern uncle were excellent friends still; the bright girlish nature was not easily quelled, and her light-hearted prattle and laughter seemed to lift the sombre cloud of severity from Sir Stephen's brow.

The tie between Philip and Lina was evidently becoming nearer and dearer as the days and months grew into years.

Mrs. Ruskett's ambitious plans were for the nonce checkmated by this increasing attachment, and the frequent interchange of visits between the cousins. Isabel, who had found Pineridge exceedingly dull, was delighted when she obtained prolonged leave of absence from her "Ma," and continued to sojourn in London with infinite satisfaction. She took up her residence with Mrs. Jane Hopkins entirely, who found her an agreeable and useful companion, for Mrs. Hopkins let lodgings to people engaged at the theatre, and Isabel was always ready to assist in looking after the lively boarders, whom she considered as quite the most delightful people she had ever met. Thus time went on, and she stayed on, knowing no greater pleasure than a surreptitious peep *behind the scenes* of the Kaleidoscope Theatre, where Mrs. Hopkins still filled the post of dresser to the leading ladies of the ballet. It had now

become the height of Miss Ruskett's
ambition to figure in a burlesque some
day, and she felt confident that thus,
and thus only, could she obtain the full
meed of admiration due to her dashing
appearance and those wicked black eyes
which the "gentlemen lodgers" in the
Waterloo Road were never tired of prais-
ing.

Mrs. Ruskett had most reluctantly resigned herself to the conviction that
nothing was to be done with the "heir-
apparent," during his repeated absences
in London. Still it gratified her to
know that her daughter remained within
easy reach of him. Better times might
come yet; but for the present she could
only play a waiting game. She therefore
resolved to offer no opposition to her
daughter's residence in the metropolis.

She was safe with Mrs. Hopkins, and her services to the lodgers paid for her board. Besides, the girl liked a town life; and that was a delightful fact, for anything was better than to have her wasting her time at the Priory, a useless occupant in the housekeeper's room, grumbling from morning till night, and causing dissension between the housekeeper and the upper servants, who all objected to that fine lady daughter of hers.

And so the years went swiftly by—uneventful, tranquil years these, to the chief actors in our domestic drama. But the mere passage of time must effect some changes, and when, after a lapse, we note its results, they seem startling, though during its actual progress we heed none of these evolutions.

The four years that have passed have given Lina the prestige of blooming seventeen, while Philip has reached the eve of his majority. During the many happy months he has spent under his uncle's hospitable roof at Hampstead, he has learned to appreciate the nature of the tie that binds him to his cousin, and Lina and he have acknowledged their true love for one another, and have resolved to spend their happy future together as man and wife. Her parents are delighted at the prospect, towards which all their hopes have so long tended, and Sir Stephen, after considerable hesitation, has at length condescended to yield his consent to the engagement of the cousins. His reluctance has been very evident, and caused the young people much heart-aching anxiety; but that is as it should be, Sir Stephen thought. Juniors should be taught patience and submission to their elders. The baronet did not at all approve of the new-fangled notions which encouraged young people to follow their own foolish ideas, and to carry them out with a reckless disregard of all the proprieties. He admired and strove to model himself after the pattern of some such stern parent as Sir Anthony Absolute, and he succeeded, but without that worthy's noisy scenes of passion and abuse. Sir Stephen upheld *decorum* above all things, and his anger was of the quiet, incisive kind, which made itself felt more effectually than any violent bluster would have done.

He disapproved of the marriage of relations on principle, and Philip's resolve to wed his cousin aroused his father's ancient grievance and disappointment anent his son's deprivation. If the youth had been as others were, he might have chosen a bride among the leading families of the county, as his position 'certainly entitled him to do ; but, owing to his helplessness, he had to content himself with the patient cousin, who was willing to accept him and his needs.

Oh ! that curse of blindness ! Sir Stephen gnashes his teeth with rage as he reverts to the aggravating subject. How it has hampered him at every step ! What a miserable sort of education it compelled him to give to the heir of Pineridge !

He had really been thankful to get the lad out of his house ; to know him in the safe custody of his aunt and her daughter.

Pretty training this for a landowner !

Music his chief delight, his only accomplishment; read to, sung to, pampered and cossetted by a pair of compassionate women. Letitia was amiable, true, generous, and upright; but she was *only* a woman, and her every-day life was moulded and guided simply by her own feminine notions of duty and right. How was it possible that she could obtain any knowledge thus, which would fit her, or her blind pupil, to cope with the world and its disciples? And yet, what career was there that Philip could follow? How could he, for instance, have been trained for any diplomatic post? How could he fulfil any public duties? His terrible infirmity unfitted him entirely for any but the most insignificant pursuits.

Lina's devotion to her cousin, and her

perfect comprehension of his manifold wants, were certainly points in her favour. And it might have been difficult to find another girl of such charming manners and appearance ready to sacrifice herself and her future to a blind man. Lina would certainly be a credit to the house of Northcroft, and there was consolation in the fact that its noble name was hers by inheritance.

Philip had gone home with an attendant to Pineridge to plead his cause, and that of the girl he loved, in person ; and when he had finally obtained his father's long-deferred consent, he returned to Hampstead, where he was received with more than usual rejoicing. The lovers young, radiant, hopeful, looked happily towards the future now, which they were to spend together. The chief, indeed the only, trouble of their past had been the periodical partings, rendered necessary by the fact of their separate homes.

Now, all this would be changed, the young couple would take up a permanent residence at the Priory, and there were times when Sir Stephen himself smiled at the prospect of having a handsome young lady as mistress of his establishment again. She was a little youthful still, and perhaps wanting in that reticence and dignity which Sir Stephen considered a *sine quâ non*, but he would undertake her training personally, and who could doubt its admirable result? Lina herself was unspeakably happy, because she saw Philip so glad, and it seemed to the grateful girl as if Providence was too good to her.

Had she not the best, kindest, most generous parents? Had not her life been all brightness and peace? and now was not the last and most ardent wish of her heart to be gratified also?

"I get frightened when I realize my intense happiness," she said to her mother just after Philip had brought the good news of his father's consent. "I feel as if something dreadful will happen; the course of true love is not supposed to run thus smoothly, is it, mother dear?"

"I hope and pray that your joy is *blessed*, my poor darling," cries Mrs. Northcroft, with intense fervour, "for it is unselfish. You have chosen the better part; you intend to devote yourself, all your hopes, pleasures, and ambition, to the undivided care of a blind man. If you fulfil the hard task you have under-

taken conscientiously, surely, surely no
evil will come to you."

Mrs. Northcroft flings her arms wildly
around the girl, and breaks into passionate sobs.

"God grant that you may be kept free
from any suffering but such as you
deserve yourself, my precious, precious
child," she cries, and suddenly relaxing
her grasp, she falls back, panting, ex-
hausted, deadly white.

Lina, alarmed, and a good deal perplexed too, by her gentle mother's
amazing vehemence, does all she can to
restore her to her usual equanimity, and
when she sees her settling down to a
peaceful sleep, the girl steals quietly away
to her lover.

"Mother is so strange," she says; "she
almost fainted just now, and she is look-

ing very ill. She will not acknowledge
it, but I am positive that it is the idea of
going to the Priory which always upsets
her now. The fact of your father's con-
senting to let our wedding take place in
Torshire will necessitate mother's going
down, of course, and I am sure the
thought of staying at Pineridge has made
her ill again. She was not herself when
last we were all down there, you know,
and we could not even persuade her to
go at all after that."

"It will be different soon, my own
darling," whispers Philip with happy conviction. "Of course dear aunt Letty
cannot feel happy, or at her ease while
my father is all alone in his chill glory
there. You wait and see how soon *we*
shall change all that. When once you
are mistress of the gloomy old home, my

sweet, bright sunshine,—gladness, peace, and content will flow within the ancient walls, and then *we* shall welcome our dear mother, and she will be happier at the Priory with her children than anywhere else in the world."

Lina accepted her lover's comforting words with hopeful eagerness, and thought less about her mother's excitement than she would have done at another time. But that touching scene had sobered the loving girl, and her buoyant anticipations were checked by the fear that Sir Stephen's courteous invitation would prove injurious to Mrs. Northcroft.

Every thing in connection with his unfortunate son was without precedent, thought the baronet ruefully, and therefore the fact of his marriage taking place at Pineridge, instead of from the house of the bride, was but another item in the whole course of the unconventional conduct of affairs, and must be accepted, like all else that was cruelly inevitable. Philip had insisted on a very quiet wedding, and here also his father had been compelled reluctantly to yield, and having done so, Sir Stephen suddenly resolved to make the best of matters, and sent his brother a very cordial invitation to spend the next month at Pineridge, and to see the young couple comfortably installed there, before he returned to Hampstead and the work awaiting him for the next year's Exhibition. Mrs. Northcroft bore the journey and the change of residence uncommonly well, and Lina rejoiced accordingly; but Hubert, who generally accepted all the arrangements made for him in a cheer-

ful and contented spirit, proved fractious
on this occasion, and seemed possessed
by an unwonted uneasiness and responsibility, which he was incapable of shaking off.

Now, to add to this, it so happened
that he would have to be followed into
Torshire by an emissary from his principal patron, the Graf von Stein, who
resided in Munich. This fact annoyed
and preoccupied the artist. He was fully
aware of Sir Stephen's unabated objection
to all the details of his profession, and
it worried him to bring these so clearly
en évidence by the visit of the Count's
major-domo, who brought a damaged
picture with him. Hubert had always
managed to laugh at his brother's absurd
prejudices, but he resented them all the
same, and had taken more pains than

even his wife gave him credit for, not to run counter to them too frequently.

The Graf von Stein had a fine picture gallery, on which he prided himself, and it really contained an admirable collection of modern paintings. Among these was the famous "Pine Forest" picture on which Hubert Northcroft had reason to pride himself. The Count had seen it at the private view of the pictures in Trafalgar Square, more than four years ago, and had then purchased it. This generally admired landscape had lately been much injured by the falling in of a portion of the glass roof of the gallery, and Graf von Stein was overwhelmed with grief at the mischief which had befallen it. The picture had received a blow in the excitement which ensued on the breaking of the roof, some of the paint was scraped off, and daylight was now actually visible through the canvas.

All this news, and more to the same effect, had been received in a letter from the noble Graf, a day or two prior to the departure from Hampstead, where Hubert had managed to prolong his tenancy. Graf von Stein was elderly and fidgety; he set a great store by his collection of pictures, and was in despair at this untoward accident.

"But it fortunately happens," wrote his Excellency to the artist, "that my confidential servant is journeying to England next month. He is a thoroughly reliable person, and I feel inclined to let him take charge of the picture, since I have determined that no hand but your own shall restore it. Will it be possible for you to undertake this matter at once, as Wolfgang's stay in England is limited, and I cannot permit him to return without my favourite picture?"

Such was the gist of Graf von Stein's elaborate epistle, in which flourishes, verbal and caligraphic, played an important part. Hubert had answered "yes" to all inquiries. Now, however, that his daughter's marriage and his brother's gracious invitation would take him to Pineridge, nothing remained for him but to request the confidential servant of his Excellency to follow him to Torshire with the extensive packing-case containing the precious work of art in question.

It was a "terrible bother," of course: but artists were always being bothered, and he must submit like the rest.

Lina made many a joke about "papa and his artistic retinue," and when "the German gentleman, with the picture," was announced, a day or two after the party had arrived at Pineridge, and the quiet preparation for the nuptials were at their height, the girl's merry laugh reached the ears of the grumbling artist, as he wended his way to the studio above. This had been left just as Mrs. Northcroft first arranged it, now more than six years back. "The German gentleman" rose with evident *empressement* as Hubert entered the studio, and, bowing, he thus delivered himself in florid German : —

"I have been desired, sir, by his Excellency, the Herr Graf von Stein, to place this picture upon your easel with my own hands, and I have pledged my

honour that no further harm shall happen
to it; therefore have I ventured to commence the unpacking immediately, but
oh! sir!—and here the wizen-faced little
foreigner threw hammer and screw-driver
aside, and spread out his arms as if
about to clasp the amazed artist to his
heart—"it is more than anxiety about
that picture which causes my emotion,"
he goes on; "it is the thought that now,
after so many years, I should have the
happiness to see you once again! You,
Meinherr, who to all appearance have
not changed at all, though you have made
so great a name for yourself, and are
so famous already, while I, alas! fill a
sphere but little superior to that in which
I had the honour of waiting upon you—
why, it must be quite fourteen years
ago!"

Hubert, looking puzzled and uneasy, waits patiently for the end of this elaborate speech, quietly wondering the while if this droll little man had had sunstroke, and what all his strange excitement portends.

"Does the *Gnädige* Herr thus entirely fail to recognise his most humble, most obedient servant, Karl Wolfgang? Has the Herr no recollection of being at Meyringen in past days? Perhaps it is the length of time which has elapsed since then, which somewhat obscures the Herr Northcroft's memory. With some persons the power of recollection is strong, with others weak. I think, though there is little I can with justice pride myself upon, that in this matter of memory I am not easily to be surpassed," continues Mr. Wolfgang, with that peculiar assurance which so often characterizes small, fussy men. "Will the gracious Mr. Painter allow me to recall to him a certain catastrophe which happened near Meyringen just at the time when the Herr, his lady, and their dear little daughter were at the hotel? And when those kind visitors proved themselves so very benevolent towards the poor orphan child of a guide, who was so brave and yet was so cruelly killed?"

Hubert suddenly begins to stuff his pipe with unwonted energy, and while Karl Wolfgang at length takes the damaged picture out of the packing-case and carefully places it upon the easel, the painter looks on with eyes that see not. Indeed, he feels like one in a dream . . . Is this the hand of fate?

Of all the myriad inhabitants of Ger-

many, why should this prying individual
have been selected to come on this mis-
sion to England?

"Father," says Lina, entering hurriedly,
" mother bade me ask you what answer
we are to send to this letter? Shall we
accept the invitation, or decline it? The
messenger waits for a reply."

As Lina crosses the studio to offer the
letter to her father, she perceives the
stranger, who is on his knees still, gather-
ing up the straw and shavings belonging
to the packing-case.

He springs to his feet now and stares
at the astonished girl with widely-opened
eyes.

"Herr Gott in Himmel!" he exclaims,
clasping his hands.

"I beg your pardon!" says Lina, gently
inclining her head as she moves towards

the door, and finding the stranger about to address her, she glances nervously back at her father, whose silence perplexes her.

"Run away, Lina, run away! cries the artist with sudden asperity. "What do you mean by interrupting me when you know I am so busy? Don't bother me about anybody's letters; leave me in peace, do."

He has risen in sudden haste and holds the door wide, so that she shall the more speedily make her exit.

   *   *   *   *   *

"Something has happened to father," says Lina, rejoining Philip, whom she has left at the piano in the drawing room. "He spoke quite crossly to me. I never knew him so strange and angry before."

She tries to laugh, but her father's extraordinary behaviour has sorely perplexed her, and she is suddenly silent.

"You are not troubled about dear old uncle's odd manner, surely, my darling?" asks Philip tenderly, and he draws her down to the chair by his side. "Why, I, even, have found out by this time that artists are wholly unaccountable people; they laugh when others cry, they bemoan what causes rejoicing to outsiders."

"Of course, dear," answers Lina gently, "it was all my fault; I interrupted father's *séance* with his patron's ambassador, by asking stupid questions about an invitation to dinner."

"Oh! is the German ambassador in the august presence?" asks Philip.

"He is, my dear, and he is the most extraordinary little fellow; he stared at me in the rudest, oddest manner, as if he knew me, or as if I had been a ghost. I assure you I felt quite un-comfortable."

"Oh, those foreigners never know their places, not the best of them don't," re-marks Mrs. Ruskett, with a virtuous sniff of indignation. She has just brought two vases filled with fresh flowers, and lingers there talking, much to the annoy-ance of the cousins, who resent the spirit of *surveillance* which leads the house-keeper to be present on one pretext or another, whenever they are enjoying a *tête-à-tête* in the drawing room.,

"My daughter Isabel is taking lessons in music and singing from one of those foreigners, now, Mr. Philip," continues the loquacious old lady, enjoying the knowledge that her presence is unwel-

come, but that neither of the young
people dare to bid her leave the room.
She resents the betrothal of the cousins
with exceeding bitterness, and revels in
the chance of causing "the young pair of
fools" any sort of annoyance. "There's
many a slip 'twixt the cup and the lip,"
she adds, lifting down a precious bit of
china from the mantel-shelf, and dusting
it with elaborate attention to its minute
crevices. "There's never any knowing
what may happen in this changeful world,
as I often say to my Isabel, and so I
often tell her to make the most of her
chances. We are but dust, and who can
foretell what a day may bring forth to
them that are ashes!"

"Play me that last bit of the *scherzo*
over again, dearest, you have not got it
quite right yet," whispers Lina, leaning

over her cousin, and placing his fingers
back on the keys.

. Philip speedily takes the hint, and
begins to play with such spirit and so
much vigour that Mrs. Ruskett finds her
further speech unintelligible, and retires
in dudgeon.

"Won't let me have my little say, now,
won't she? And is jealous of my even
mentioning my Isabel, too, that's very
evident. And so the little foreigner
stared at her as if he knew her, did he?
What does that mean? She looked quite
'ot, and seemed awfully put out like.
And her father was cross, was he? I
wonder if there's anything amiss? If
there is, it will not be long before *I* find
it out, that's certain, trust me for that, or
my name is not Sarah Ruskett. I'll invite
the German gentleman to have a chop

and a glass of port in my room, and I'll find out the reason of his staring. Perhaps he's seen her with some lover the forward minx picked up in London, and now her father is on the scent, she's frightened, and so she takes time by the forelock, and gets Mr. Philip to hear her side of the story first. Ah! she's that artful, is Miss Lina; just like the rest of those fair-haired girls, quiet and deep she is, real wicked deep, I believe. London is an awful tempestuous place for young ladies, that I'm quite sure of, and if it weren't for this botheration of a wedding, I'd get my girl home, and keep her safe under my eye, that I would. But now to hear what this foreigner's staring means. There's more than meets the eye, I can tell that by young Miss's flurry."

Thus Mrs. Ruskett soliloquizes as she

slowly traverses the hall, and makes her way back to her own apartments.

Before another hour is over, she has given Mr. Wolfgang meat and wine, and has been so startled by that illustrious foreigner's conversation, that she actually requests a private audience of her austere master, who, surprised, and by no means willingly, grants her the ten minutes she asks for, as she intercepts him on his return from hunting late that afternoon.

Lina and Philip meanwhile continue their practice at the piano, play their duets, sing their songs, and occasionally forget all about the music in their sweet lovers' talk of the happy future now coming nearer and nearer.

" Before this week is over you will be my wife, Lina; my own, own, precious darling wife," says Philip, and he takes her soft little hands into his long clinging pressure, and then he draws her bodily into his close embrace.

"My love, my sunshine," he says, "how good God has been to us! How happy and grateful we ought to be! You love me, all blind and helpless as I am, and you do know at least that I can never fail in absolute devotion to you. Your pleasure must be my law, for I can never know any other. As you lead me I am bound to follow; as you bid me I must perforce obey. And it will be my joy, and pride, and delight, to prove myself your most obedient slave. Your nature is so tender, too, my darling, that my affliction gives me an additional claim on your generous love, and every day that passes proves to me, more and more thoroughly, how well we are suited to one another. Is not this true?"

She is standing by his side now, her arm laid lovingly around his neck; her earnest eyes seem gazing far, far, into the distant but surely happy future. They make a charming picture, these happy lovers. He with his slender hands upon the keyboard, his head uplifted, the sightless eyes closed instinctively, for he is listening to the last faint echo of the final chord he has just played. She, tall, supple, and gracefully formed, with an air of dignity and courage in her aspect, as she stands wondering and waiting, what her heart's lord may please to say or require next.

Lina has now grown to perfect womanhood, and she presents a picture of purity but seldom seen in this last decade, which has been rampant with " girls of the period," " professional beauties," " society startlers," &c. Our Lina cannot be accounted as strictly beautiful, an irregularity of feature prevents that ; but there is a combination of everything that is true, honest, and good, in the expression of her mobile, sensitive face. If lovely can be construed as lovable, then Lina decidedly merits the pleasing adjective.

" Play me that introduction again, dearest, " she says, placing his fingers upon the keys, " I feel I could sing the prayer now. The daylight is dying, and ' *Leise, leise,*' is most appropriate."

Philip plays the opening chords of the famous recitative that ushers in the well-known prayer of " Der Freischütz," and is followed by the grand air of the opera.

This *scena* Lina sings better and more effectively than any of the others that constitute her well-selected *répertoire*. Herr Lirtz had always spoken of his pupil's rendering of this lovely " Freischütz " music with enthusiastic approbation, and had even told Miss Northcroft that she could hold an audience spell-bound if she would ever thus sing in public. But Philip is all the audience Lina desires, and his delighted approval is worth far more to her than the plaudits of a multitude of strangers could ever be. Now her voice rises, clear, full, melodious, and she delivers the difficult passage at the end of the recitative with masterly clearness and precision that does all honour to the able teaching of Herr Lirtz, as well as to the musical ability of his favourite pupil.

Then she breathes the softly inspired notes of the prayer, and all unconsciously she clasps her hands in entreaty.

"Lina, your voice is what one dreams the voice of an angel must be," cries Philip, rising at the conclusion of the *andante* and flinging his arms tenderly about his betrothed. "Darling, we must certainly journey to the Rhineland together, and the Black Forest, too. I always associate the sombre shades of that mysterious Schwartzwald with all the weird doings of Kaspar, Rudolf, and the incantation scene. Shall we go abroad next spring? Do you think my young wife will be able to undertake the difficult charge of so troublesome a burden as her husband will be to her?"

And so they prattle, and play, and sing in happy alternation; light-hearted and content, knowing no evil, fearing none. It is Mr. Grind's entry with the lamp which first warns Lina of the passage of time; for she suddenly becomes aware that twilight has deepened into darkness.

"Has Sir Stephen returned from hunting?" she asks the butler. And when he has replied in the affirmative, "I must hurry away to help mother to dress for dinner," she says to Philip, "and I shall be late too."

"We were so taken up with our music, we never heard the gong," he replies in half apology to the butler, whom he fears to some extent.

"We certainly did not heed it," says Lina, unabashed. She quails as little before the butler as before his austere master. "Take my arm, Philip," she says, "let me lead you upstairs."

They cross the hall arm in arm, and when they reach the upper landing—

"Give me my good-night's kiss now, darling," pleads Philip; "you know I never get any but a formal salutation when my father and the rest of them are present."

"Well then, good-night, sweetheart, good-night," she says earnestly. "Meanwhile I hope you will enjoy your dinner none the less for receiving your good-night kiss beforehand."

"Good-bye, sweetheart, good-bye!"— answers Philip, singing the words; but just as he is turning away in the direction of his room, a sudden impulse of overwhelming tenderness possesses him, as he stands waiting, his arms outstretched. "Lina, my own love, my life, my wife!" he cries as he snatches her close to his throbbing heart, and then, with a strange, anxious expression, " You will never leave me, never forsake me, my precious treasure?" he whispers. His voice sounds almost as though there is a sob in it.

"Thy people shall be my·people, thy God my God!" she answers, and the sweet lips pressed upon his seem to set a fresh seal upon the lasting bond between them.

Do presentiments exist? are subtle warnings given to mortals of the evils advancing towards them? Was there not something more than the lover's ardour beating unrecognised in Philip's anxious heart, as he clasped his betrothed in his arms again and again, and seemed so loth to let her go from him?

CHAPTER XII

L INA hurries to her mother's room con-
trite and apologetic for having tarried
so long. It is the daughter's pleasant task
to act as lady's-maid to her gentle mother
every evening.

But Mrs. Northcroft is not in her room.
And the satin dinner-dress has been taken
from the bed. Can she have dressed alone
and gone downstairs already? Strange that
Lina did not meet her on the landing or in
the hall below. The girl knocks hurriedly
at the door of her father's dressing-room.
No reply. He also has decended ; but his
candles are burning, and his dress-clothes
are laid ready upon the chest of drawers.

Something has happened!

The routine of the Priory household has never been thus perturbed before. Can Sir Stephen have met with an accident in the hunting field? Lina's heart beats loud and fast as she flies downstairs, and in the hall she comes into sudden and violent collision with Mrs. Ruskett, whose head is in startling proximity to the handle of the library door. This gives Lina her clue. Something *has* happened, and her parents are in Sir Stephen's room in consultation. Without a word to the startled house keeper, Miss Northcroft passes her, and opening the door of the library, she closes it rapidly and firmly again as soon as she has entered the room.

*   *   *   *   *

Her mother is there. She is already

dressed for dinner. Is it the peculiar shade of the reading lamp, or the dark sheen of her high satin gown, which makes her look so awfully ill, so ghastly pale? Lina runs towards her, but is checked by an imperious movement from her uncle's hand as he stands facing her, white and rigid also. His mud-bespattered hunting-coat, and his dirty top-boots are strangely at variance with the excessive neatness of his surroundings. Instinctively Lina turns to look for her father.

He stands apart, he appears puzzled and disturbed, but not frightened as his wife is.

"What has happened, uncle Stephen? What is wrong?" asks Lina promptly. Her straightforward nature abhors doubt and uncertainty, and she desires to break this ominous, perplexing silence at once.

"It is as well you have come at this moment, Lina," replies the baronet, "for what transpires here is likely to prove as important to you as to myself. I have been compelled — reluctantly compelled, I may say, to request the immediate presence and attention of my brother and his wife, because I have a question of vital consequence to put to them." There is a strange vibration in his chilling tones, and most unusual hesitation in his measured speech.

"What does this portend?" Lina glances from one to the other of the white faces in growing alarm. "Whatever question you have to put to my dear parents," she says proudly, "I am certain will be answered to your immediate satisfaction, uncle Stephen." She has been stung by the odd way in which he alluded to my "brother and his wife!"

"I trust your childish confidence may not be misplaced, Lina," he says coldly; "and I admit that the proposition which has just been laid before me is so astounding, as to appear incredible even to me. In any case, I have no alternative but to place the facts before you, as they have been reported to me. I admit that the duplicity they imply is monstrous, and I shall await an explanation with exceeding anxiety."

There is a long, trying pause. The ticking of the Queen Anne clock upon the mantelshelf assumes the magnitude of blows from a sledge-hammer to the overstrained sense of hearing of those in solemn conclave assembled.

At last Sir Stephen breaks the awful silence, and moving a step nearer to Mrs.

Northcroft, he addresses himself pointedly to her—

" Your extraordinary depression, your failing health, your white, troubled face, and evident disinclination to be my guest, lend more colour to the fatal suspicion that has been whispered to me than aught else. If what I have heard be true, then, Mrs. Northcroft, your mysterious fretting and lasting nervousness are amply accounted for. Indeed, it is a marvel to me that any one could live under so crushing a load of falsehood and deceit." The lurid flame of a fierce, growing anger shines in his eyes, and he raises his fist as though in menace.

Letitia's head falls forward upon her breast, and she shrinks as if a blow had actually been dealt her.

" Hubert—husband, come to me ! help

me!" she cries, in a tone of piteous
appeal. Hubert starts forward, the perplexed expression of his face increased to
absolute bewilderment as he listens to his
brother's amazing tirade.

"It is all right, all right, Letty, my
poor darling," he whispers, taking her
ice-cold hands in his, and chafing them
nervously. "Stephen does not mean to
be angry, dear, it is only his manner.
We can explain it all, of course."

"Oh! we were wrong, so wrong to
keep it secret for all these years," she
whispers faintly, and only her husband
hears her. "I have always dreaded this
moment, dear Hugh, and that is why I
so often implored you to tell——"

"Tut—tut—much ado about nothing,
my poor child," answers Hubert cheerily,
and then he faces his brother.

" What has put you out so much, Stephen ? " he says, and his tone is nearly as calm as usual. " Come, come, we are not acting a play—we don't want heroics or hysterics either. What is all this—fuss about ? "

" Your flippant, irreverent tone at this most serious moment is in as bad taste as all the other acts of your frivolous *Bohemian* existence, Hubert," says Sir Stephen, with bitter sarcasm. " But this frivolity in you can no longer deceive me, and I see the confirmation of my worst suspicions in the scared face of that guilty woman, who cowers under the exposure that has come upon her—only just in time! But it *is* in time, thank God ! "

" Uncle, be silent : how can you ? " cries Lina, suddenly confronting him, and striving to silence him by the imperious gesture of her uplifted hand. " You are hurting mother. Don't you see that she is ill? How dare you speak to her in that cruel way?" The girl rushes towards Mrs. Northcroft, and tenderly pillows the drooping head upon her loving breast. "Mother—mother darling—are you faint—let me get your salts—oh! what can I do for her?" cries poor Lina, in a tone of despair.

" *Mother!* " echoes the baronet with contempt. "Don't *you* know that that woman is not your mother, girl, any more than the man I am compelled to call brother is your father?"

"Oh, uncle; how *can* you?" protests Lina.

But he is too much roused to have either mercy or consideration for any one. His pride, his prejudices, his sense of the fitness of things, all have suffered, and

he resents the cause of his bitter humilia-
tion. "You were picked up in a gutter
—a pauper, with no parents, and no
name—and *you* have sought to entrap
my son, the heir of Pineridge, the bearer
of a noble name, into a marriage! Our
of this house all of you—adventuresses—
cheats—impostors—out of my house!"

"What you say is *not* true—none of
it—I'll not believe it," cries Lina, with
passionate revolt mingling in her amaze-
ment; "and Philip will not believe ill
of us either,—of that I am quite sure!
Oh, my love, my darling," she murmurs
below her breath. The thought of *him*
gives her fresh strength, and her earnest
conviction actually shakes Sir Stephen
but he turns fiercely towards his brother.

"Is this girl entitled to bear the
noble name of Northcroft?" he cries

"Is she your own daughter? Answer me that. Yes—or no?"

"Why, Stephen, Stephen, what is the use of making such a fuss?" rejoins Hubert helplessly. He really is bewildered by the strange aspect of affairs. "Certainly we adopted little Lisbeth, and re-christened her Lina when our own baby was taken from us. She is the child of excellent, worthy people. Her father won a noble name for *himself* by his bravery and courage. Don't put yourself out so much, brother. It's all right, I assure you. I told my wife not to bother you with all these details: it's entirely my fault that you did not know, and, after all, who could fail to be proud of our Lina? We have loved and treated her as if she had been our own child, of course."

" Silence, liar and cheat ! " roars Sir Stephen. The concentrated rage of his suspicious nature finds vent in his furious tones. " Out of my house without a moment's delay. No more tampering with that wretched blind boy. Out, and at once ! "

He crosses the room with hasty strides; he places his hand on the bell-rope, and pulls it violently.

" Run to the stables, have the horses put to, and say that the carriage is required immediately. Tell Mr. Grind to have all the luggage belonging to Mr. Hubert Northcroft and his family brought down at once. They start for London by the mail-train to-night."

" But dinner, sir——" stammers the astonished footman, who is young, and has no experience in hiding his emotions.

" Dinner be——, and you also ! " shouts the master of Pineridge, in a white heat of passion by this time.

* * * * *

Within an hour, Hubert, his wife, and Lina are driving rapidly along the road to Torchester.

Within two hours they are *en route* for London, borne rapidly through the chill, dark night, by the whizzing express train. . . . . . Onward, onward flies the engine, breathing sparks of fire in its hot haste. It is close upon midnight ; the wretched hours of this most eventful, most miserable day have almost come to an end. Letitia Northcroft, with a sigh, has laid her white face wearily upon her husband's shoulder, and has given her ice-cold hands into Lina's warm, loving clasp.

"Take care of *him*, my darling," she whispers, roused by some temporary stoppage of the train, and then she lays her husband's hands in those of her adopted child, and with a long sigh suddenly breathes her last! The shock has killed her, as Sir Joseph Barry prophesied a shock would do. Her gentle heart is broken, the firm support of her courageous love and never-failing moral strength are taken from poor Hubert now, and he is left, a widower indeed! crushed in spirit, paralyzed by the grief which has so fearfully and unexpectedly overwhelmed him. Instinctively he turns to Lina, and he does not turn in vain. The brave child realizes that this is no time for indulgence in private sorrow or repining. She must ignore herself entirely, she will exert all the latent energy of her strong, simple nature, and prove herself worthy of the love and trust which have been bestowed upon her throughout the past happy years of her glad young life, as completely as if she had been really entitled to the name she bears. She will reward that gentle woman, who has been to her all that a mother can be to a daughter, by taking the burden of Hubert's crushing sorrows upon her own strong shoulders. She will be firm as a rock, and show herself able and willing to support this sad, broken-spirited man ; she is resolved, by the gracious help of her Father in heaven, to prove to her earthly parent that he will not lean upon the child of his adoption in vain.

END OF VOL. I.

www.ingramcontent.com/pod-product-compliance
Lightning Source LLC
Chambersburg PA
CBHW030618030726
47497CB00006B/1548